ELMER

NO ORDINARY WOLF

Paul Lindley

ISBN: 978-0-244-31005-9

PublishNation
www.publishnation.co.uk

In fond memory of Max, Leo and Buster.

"Until you have truly loved an animal part of your soul never awakens."

TABLE OF CONTENTS

MORNING HAS BROKEN

THE NEIGHBOURS

THE DENSITE

LIFE IS PRECIOUS

WATER, LIFE GIVER AND LIFE TAKER

FAMILY FIRST

ACCEPTANCE

NEAR MISS

ORIN

THE GOOD LIFE

THE FIRST HUNT

MORE LESSONS IN LIFE

HUNTING SCHOOL

IT'S NOT ALL PLAY

HOW QUICKLY THE TABLES CAN BE CHANGED

SIGNS OF OTHERS

THE LYNX

LIVING WITH RAVENS

THE BEAR

DANGER IS NEVER FAR AWAY

WINTER IS COMING

THE SNOW

THE FIRST REAL HUNT IN THE SNOW

FAMILY IS EVERYTHING

TRIALS OF LIFE

BROTHERLY LOVE

LIFE IS NEVER EASY

THE OTTER

LADY LUCK

THE SECOND DENSITE

NEW LIFE COMES AND GOES

CONTEMPLATION

CHAPTER 1

MORNING HAS BROKEN

It was a huge oak, truly ancient, standing tall and alone among a forest of much younger beech and birch: apart from the very earth itself all around was young in comparison.

The large black wolf had spent the night resting beneath the wide umbrella of the trees natural protection, and he now gazed upwards with a sort of admiration for this giant above him. Finger like rays of golden sunlight were finding their way through the gaps in the trees spring foliage, some landing on the back of the dozing wolf and warming his dark coat quickly.

He rolled over onto his side and laid there motionless for a few seconds. Almost without thought his long legs stretched outwards, four huge paws pushing to their furthest extent, as if trying to touch something just beyond their reach. He waited for the sleepy muscles throughout the rest of his body to join in, just like they always did, and his whole body shuddered. All this time, a slow constantly wagging tail told of his inner pleasure.

A slow, twisting jerk of his body took him onto his back, and with all four legs pointing skywards he wriggled around violently, as if trying to scratch an itch in the centre of his back. He enjoyed the feelings and pondered whether to rise to his feet or stay where he was.

Elmer rose slowly to his feet and carried out another full body stretch, sliding his front paws through the dirt in front of him while keeping his back ones still, his back then arching skywards in a final measured movement. He returned to a normal standing position. Quiet and completely still the wolf concentrated hard for a few minutes, opening up his impressive senses to their fullest, accepting the signs of Mother Nature all around him as they flooded in. The strong, fragrant smells from flowering Bluebells, Wild Daffodils and garlicky Ramsons, all indicators of his ancient woodland home, permeated his sensitive nose. His ears listened intently for anything of note, while golden eyes peered deep into the hidden depths of the forest all about him. Happy all was well he shook the whole of his body with great vigour, just like he did when drying himself after leaving the water. Any lingering signs of sleepiness now forced from his body he was ready to go.

The behaviour of the wolf had been watched intently by a small squirrel, sat safely out of reach beside her high rise home; a converted magpies nest. The orangey red rodent began chattering away loudly, anticipating the movement of this formidable forest predator, but Elmer didn't leave straight away. He remained standing there, bushy tail swishing slowly from side to side. His huge head turned slightly to one side, allowing an obvious gaze of contentment to fall on the still resting wolf beside him.

The sleek huntress was called Freya. Until recently, she had been the fastest member of another distant wolf family. Like Elmer, Freya was also three years old. Totally grey, apart from a small white patch on her chest, she was easy to tell from others for she had a prominent kink half way down her tail. Her light build gave great speed, something which she and her new mate now often relied on.

Freya remained lying. She returned her partners gaze as her powerfully wagging tail swept the forest floor around behind her; telling too of her own contentment with the present situation. She cast her hunters eyes over her mate, admiring his size and the great strength that she knew he had. At 150 pounds he was almost twice her weight, amongst the largest and strongest of their kind. He had other qualities too though, one's that attracted her more than just his size alone.

Elmer was a noble wolf she thought: brave and courageous, loyal and unwavering, one that would lead with fairness and compassion. Freya never felt the need to become submissive before him and he had never asked this of her. Her own parents had ruled their pack using aggression and fear, it was her mother who had given her that kink in her tail; when younger Freya had been too fast to catch and chastise, often just her disappearing tail was caught, leaving her with the obvious crick that she now and always would carry.

2

Elmer stood tall and strong beside his partner as he peered down intensely into her golden eyes. She accepted his stare with a wide open welcome and Elmer found himself thinking deeply about his life so far, the events that had brought them together; he cast his mind back...................

Born into a small but strong pack with parents that were both six years old, Elmer was one of five pups. He had two older juvenile brothers and two adult sisters to help look after him. Elmer's father was a wolf of great stature too, strong and always courageous. His mother was fast, sometimes furious, but always fair. He could not have had better parents, and they taught him well.

Elmer's early life went much like many other wolfs, there were times of great happiness and great sadness, of ease and hardship, triumph and tragedy. At a young age he lost one of his brothers to a snake bite. Just a month later, one of his sisters was gored by a rampaging boar, a result of inexperience and youthful enthusiasm; she died two weeks later. As a juvenile a third litter mate, another brother, was killed by other wolves.

Like all of his birth pack Elmer mourned the loss of any of it's members greatly. He watched his mighty father grieve with every loss, sometimes for days. Family was everything to the wolf, Elmer knew this for that feeling was inside of him, and because his parents showed him this was their way.

By three years old Elmer had grown into a wolf to be reckoned with, larger, stronger and equally as brave as his father, he was often the telling factor when hunting larger prey. Throughout those early years Elmer had always taken it upon himself to watch over any new pups that joined his fathers family, it was in his nature to do so. Elmer thought the world of all his birth pack but always harboured extra strong feelings for his father.

Thoughts about leaving his family had been troubling him for many weeks. Like most wolves Elmer was being motivated by his genes, that all powerful urge to breed, to have a pack and home of his own; it was so very strong. Some young wolves might leave their birth pack at an age much younger than three, driven to do so by the outside pressures from a lack of prey to feed all the family, or by the actions of other wolves. It wasn't any of these other influences that drove Elmer, it was his own body.

The feelings within him had grown more compelling by the day, spurring him on to leave and find his own way in life, but almost as powerful were the thoughts about the future welfare of his birth family. His father, now nine years old, was still an impressive wolf, but Elmer worried about the protection of his pack and their land when he was gone, his leaving would greatly reduce their strength. Eventually though, the forces of nature deep down within him won out.

Elmer gave his father that look, trotting over to bury his head deep into his side. His father sniffed in hard, soaking up the smells of his favourite son. The young wolf then wandered around the rest of his family, nudging them and sniffing in deeply, receiving the same back. Finally Elmer spent a little time with his mother, admiring the one that had brought him into this world, and hoping that one day he might find himself a partner just like her. He took one long last look towards his father, then turned and trotted purposefully away.

He was only a mile from his family when his fathers first searching howls reached his ears. Stopping for a moment he listened to the familiar sounds, his ears soon picking out the howls of others, as his mother and then the rest of his pack joined in. He didn't answer.

The next three days passed quickly, Elmer covering many miles and eating little. He constantly scented the land and the air while moving, sniffing continuously, searching for the sign of another, one who might also be looking to start a family, to join him and find a territory of their own.

This one scent was strong, it belonged to the breeding male of a resident pack. Elmer had entered a land that belonged to others and his wolf senses were telling him the family here was large. He would spend some time moving around on the fringes of their land and see if there might be a breeding female amongst them, one willing to leave with him, care would have to be taken though, he was indeed a big, powerful wolf, but he was also completely alone.

Lone travelling wolves rarely marked properly as they moved around, especially when in the territory of others, but Elmer was different, assured in his own capabilities he marked regularly on prominent places around the edges of this land, and it didn't go unnoticed.

Elmer watched from afar as the breeding male and some of his pack found his sign. His markings told them much: his sex, size, age, status and how long ago he was there. Elmer watched them become agitated, moving around with uncertainty, all except for one small female. She stood still and looked hard in his direction, unable to actually see him, but still she stared, fixated, knowing somehow that he was there.

The breeding male marked the area furiously before heading back deeper into the safety of his own territory, his pack in tow. As they headed away the small female at the back of the file turned her head, looking back over her shoulder, more than once. Elmer was interested. Over the next few days he risked marking further into the resident packs territory.

This morning, Elmer was stood on top of a large hillock. The big black wolf stared hard at the five others of his kind, travelling in single file along the valley floor below him. They stopped and all turned his way. Elmer wanted to be seen.

The breeding male took a few steps towards him, stopping and scenting the air heavily, then staring hard towards him. Elmer expected the pack leader to come after him with his family, but he didn't. The small female was at the rear again, she hadn't taken her eyes off him either, but she was looking at him with different intent.

The slender wolf left her family line and took a few steps towards the lone wolf, stopping briefly to look back at her father and the rest of her pack. It was the shortest of goodbyes. Seconds later she was off. Covering the steep ground quickly and easily she was soon coming to a halt only yards before Elmer. The two exchanged looks as scents and body language silently said it all. Her family stayed where they were, watching as the black wolf turned and headed away from them. Elmer left their land to find one of his own, the small female trotting closely behind him. Her name was Freya.

5

The harsh loud warning crows of a raven pierced the air and Elmer was snapped abruptly from his memories, back into the present day......................

Elmer lifted his stare from his partners golden eyes and searched the trees for the offending bird. These huge, alert black birds often served as a good early warning system and Elmer always took notice of them. This individual was well known to him, one that regularly dogged the pair of wolves in the hope of scraps from their table. Elmer watched him closely for a moment, quickly coming to the conclusion that his raucous calls today were just ones of high jinx. Freya had risen to her feet beside him, adding her own incredible wolf senses to the search, but like Elmer had soon realised nothing was amiss, and relaxed again.

Occasionally, when all was quiet, Elmer sometimes played with this particular raven, an ancient game it seemed to him, one of harassment by the raven and chase by the wolf. Something in the back of his mind told him this behaviour had always gone on between wolf and raven, that they were in some way connected; but the big bird never played such games with Freya. Ravens and other feathered creatures took much from the wolfs table and she had never been able to accept it.

Watched closely by Elmer, Freya carried out her own leisurely stretches before stepping across and burying her head deeply into the side of her strong and unmoving partner. She took a couple of further steps over to the huge trunk of the big old oak tree and rubbed her body fiercely on it's heavily knurled bark. As she stepped back from the tree Elmer could see the dense, light coloured mark all down her side, left by the mustard powder lichen that smothered the bark of many old oaks.

Freya could feel her coat starting to shed with the onset of the warmer weather and would use anything hard and rough that nature might provide, to help it on its way. Sometimes whole sheets of the upper fur would come away giving the appearance of looking dishevelled, but it was only a temporary thing.

The pair of wolves would be regular visitors to this old tree and many others like it in their land; later in the year mature oaks and beech would be dropping their acorns and beechnuts to the ground.

Through autumn and early winter the trees fruits would be sought out by many of the forests creatures, especially wild boar and deer, their favourite prey. Other smaller mammals and birds would also be attracted to the trees to forage at their feet, sifting through the leaf litter in search of the fat laden nuts. These smaller animals would make a welcome snack for a hungry wolf, if they could catch them.

Elmer trotted over to a smaller, smooth barked beech tree. The resident squirrel above looked on inquisitively and fell quiet. Raising one of his back legs until almost toppling over, Elmer left his mark as high as possible, for all to see and smell. After urinating he scuffed up the ground around it with powerful backward swipes of all four feet; the disturbed ground would leave a further visual sign of his presence to any interested passer-by, at the same time powerful story telling pheromones were deposited on the ground from the glands found between his toes. All these signs added to the message that this place was his. Standing tall, with tail wagging broadly from side to side, he set off at a pace that could be kept up easily all day. This morning was a good one, he thought.

As the only female Freya did some marking of her own before setting off. Squatting slightly and with a small raise of one leg she urinated close too, but not over Elmer's mark; a reinforcement of their bond. Marking finished she trotted off at a brisker pace to catch up, taking her place behind him in single file.

The territory that they had picked out for themselves was well forested and bounded on the two opposite ends by much larger packs, warranting care when travelling on its fringes, something they didn't do that often yet. The other two longer sides had natural boundaries of a large, shallow, fast flowing river on one side, and a small range of low mountains on the other; both offering a bit of an obstacle to less interested wolves. The natural barriers of river and mountains on opposite sides served to funnel some travelling prey through their land, one about twenty miles wide and thirty long.

The canopy of their home was a mix of oak, beech, birch and yew with a tiny scattering of juniper and lime trees. Lower down a good mix of woodland flowers could be found: Sorrel, Primrose, Bluebells, Snowdrops and Oxlip, all early starters, were prevalent, with later ground hugging grasses, ferns, heathers, lichens and mosses in abundance; the staple foods of deer, their main prey. Roe, Fallow, and the more impressive Red deer could all be found within their territory. The lowland Red deer that moved through their land were a little bigger than their highland cousins and the stags a quite formidable prey animal for two wolves, but the great combination of Freya's cunning and speed, with Elmer's brute strength and courage, were a perfect match. On occasion though, when Elmer was sure of a real weakness within them, he would take a large stag on his own.

Other prey to be found in their homeland included the wild boar, another favourite of theirs, but they mostly only targeted the young and juveniles, the mature adults were strong, very aggressive and well armed. Rabbits and hares were also abundant in the meadows that fringed their wooded areas, sometimes playing a major part in feeding the opportunistic wolf. At certain times of the year berries and fruit could also be found, still a source of food for a struggling wolf. All in all it was a good territory and one well worth defending.

The pair of wolves moved confidently through their beautiful, sunlit woodland, it was new, but already well known to them. Golden rays of light filtered down through the forest, landing on dew covered cobwebs, making them glisten and sparkle as the suspended liquid reflected it's light. Over the night time hard working little spiders had diligently strung the beautiful silk like nets across the woodland paths in the hope of catching insects the next day. As Elmer and his partner broke through those delicate structures, they knew they were the first to come this way.

Elmer stopped abruptly and raised his nose high into the air, sniffing hard in different directions, he had caught a familiar scent on the wind. Freya froze behind him and raised her nose to the air too, several paces behind she was not yet getting the scent. Her partner tightened his body, lowered his head, and took off at a brisk trot, a look of seriousness setting in about him. She followed and the scent that was driving him now reached her. They had not been in this territory long but they already knew the routes that many of its creatures took.

Elmer's speed hastened with ever increasing enthusiasm as he neared his destination. He left the woodland path and made his way through the brush, following a route that was only obvious to one like him. They reached a small clearing about thirty yards across and he stopped. Elmer stood motionless on the edge of the clearing his stare fixed and facing forwards, senses immediately picking up on the buzzing of extra insect life in this sunnier opening.

In just a few seconds three large Red deer stags barrelled into the clearing from the opposite side. Almost immediately the deer knew something was there. All three stopped as quickly as they could and froze on the spot.

Elmer watched them closely. The strong early morning light was landing on them, silhouetting their bodies against the darkness of the thicker forest behind, but more importantly to Elmer, hindering slightly their vision. White clouds of hot heavy breath escaped from the stag's open mouths, floating around and hanging suspended in the cool crisp morning air for a while, before melting away. The scene for a battle was set.

All three deer were mature adult animals in top condition and they stood their ground eyeing up the large black wolf before them. If they ran the wolf would follow and they might become prey, but these three had no intention of running, especially from just one wolf. An ancient test of wills between prey and hunter was about to ensue.

Elmer closed slightly but quickly on the deer in an attempt to pressurize them and find out more, a tell of weakness perhaps or maybe get them to run, but they had decided to stand. The largest of the three lowered his velvet covered antlers to browse on some lichen, not in hunger but in an attempt to influence the wolfs thinking: to try and convince the predator that he thought little of his presence.

Freya, unnoticed, had already retreated back into the woods and was busy making her way slowly and quietly around to the rear of the deer, she moved in a large circle on the downwind side to avoid the detection of her scent.

Concentrating on the large black wolf before them the three stags were unaware of her, she was truly a huntress of great skill, but these fit healthy stags would be a real test for the two of them; if they did decide to take them on.

As she closed Freya was stopped dead in her tracks. Her pupils narrowed and her eyes zoomed in on another much smaller deer standing well back behind the other stags. He was a younger adolescent male, hanging back in the shadows, watching the scene before him. The pretender had been tagging along in the hope of learning something from these more impressive, older males. Freya switched her attention to him, sure in the knowledge that Elmer would be able to work out what was happening and join her quickly, for this young stag, though smaller and less well armed, was still a formidable and dangerous adversary for her alone.

The young male deer was somehow entranced as he watched the dramatic scene unfolding before him, and totally unaware of the skilled killer approaching from his rear. Freya got as close as she dare before rushing the distracted youngster, delivering a quick slicing bite to his rear underside before he could properly react.

The three stags swung their heads round, their large antlers rattling noisily as they clashed with some of the lower branches around them. They could now make out the second wolf and not sure if there might be more quickly took stock of the changing situation. The biggest male rapidly made up his mind and with a defiant snort charged off away from Elmer. His two comrades followed suit, not wanting to waste time with any gesture towards the wolf they fled the same way, trampling the forest vegetation beneath them; the young male left to his fate.

Elmer worked out almost immediately what was happening, he knew his partner must have found something else to have a go at, and the well muscled wolf exploded off in her direction. It took a second or two for his eyes to adapt to the lower light of the partly canopied forest, but he was soon on the heels of Freya and the fleeing young stag. The dense virgin undergrowth made hard work of getting close to the deer, to snap at its hindquarters and hamstrings, Freya had to use all of her speed and skill to inflict snatched bites to the deer's rear end, while Elmer kept close to keep more pressure on, knowing that when the young male did finally come to a halt his greater strength would come into play.

Both wolves were surprised at how quickly the young stag started to tire. The initial surprise attack by Freya had dealt a deadly blow, the deep slashing bite had severed an artery and a trail of bright red blood now followed the fleeing deer through the undergrowth. A few more minutes of continual harassment, glancing strikes and large blood loss, brought the young male deer to a halt: he turned to face his pursuers.

The air was filled with the sound of the deer's heavy, erratic breathing, and a look of dread took over his wide eyes. The young male had no time to focus as Elmer hit him hard with his full weight, the force of it pushing the exhausted deer backwards, dislodging his footing. Elmer took full advantage, grabbing the young deer by the neck and dragging him down easily. Freya quickly added her weight and flashing teeth to the struggle, to help keep him down, but the young male deer already had no fight left in him. The initial burst of adrenalin had long evaporated, the huge blood loss had sapped his life force, and with the shock now set in his fate was sealed.

This was a fine meal and would last them for several days, but it had not gone unnoticed.

CHAPTER TWO

THE NEIGHBOURS

The familiar raven had followed the pair of hunters from the oak tree that morning. He was now sat high in a tall tree overlooking the feeding pair, eager for his chance to grab some for himself, but he would have to wait for Freya to have her fill and move away, for she would surely make a meal of him too, given the chance.

The raven was keeping unnaturally quiet so as not to advertise the carcass below, behaviour not normal for ravens, but he had learnt it was beneficial to him. Today it wasn't working though. All ravens watched each other, and some younger ones soaring in the vicinity had been somehow attracted by this lone raven, sat in silence atop the large beech tree; it was in their nature to take a look. Within minutes there was a growing mob of noisy birds circling the area and dropping down into the trees around the kill. This obvious bird behaviour had caught the distant and curious eyes of another deadly hunter.

These golden eyes belonged to another wolf, the breeding female from a neighbouring pack, and she was not alone. Accompanied by two of her male yearlings that were already both bigger than her, she now made a guarded beeline to the distant sign of food, her brethren in tow.

The intruders had been sat on the side of a distant hill looking over the forest laid out before them when the keen eyed female had seen the distant gathering of winged scavengers. Well aware that this was out of her own territory she had thought for a while about her actions. The top breeding female of a large powerful pack, a growing pack and one that in the future might need more space she had decided to have a closer look. Signs of food, intrigue about the new neighbouring male, and thoughts of future territory expansion were driving her; but she would have to be careful.

Elmer and Freya had eaten their fill, over forty pounds of meat had been gorged down between them and they were now resting a short distance from the kill. Freya had been leaving this spot regularly to see off the invading scavengers, the huge black ravens had now been joined by much smaller crows, piebald magpies, and a pair of hungry buzzards; Freya hated them all. Full almost to bursting point though she was quickly losing interest in the rushing back and forth, and gave up on it to lie beside her partner.

In colder and harsher times the wolves would have quickly torn large pieces from the carcass and buried them in a cache for later, but in this hotter weather it would spoil quickly. Today they would just relax and let their swollen stomachs return to normality.

Both Elmer and Freya's heads rose in unison on hearing the alarm calls of a distant green woodpecker. The loud, high pitched screeching call of the observant insect eater picrced the air, it's calls were often the first to be heard in the woods to warn of an approach. The moveable ear flaps of both wolves swivelled towards the growing array of sounds. More fleeing birds were tuning up, and red squirrels began chirping loudly. Something was approaching them and in unison, they rose to their feet, facing in it's direction. Both wolves scanned the forest depths before them, pushing their already straining senses even further.

There was no scent on the air, this and the ever nearer alarm calls told them that the advancing intruder was almost certainly another hunter. Elmer and Freya knew the threat was real now, whatever it was would have known they had entered a resident packs land, and yet they still advanced, getting closer all the time. It called for drastic action. Elmer and Freya started regurgitating most of the meat they had just eaten, emptying their stomachs to allow for faster, easier movement. Elmer in front, they moved off towards the threat.

This was their territory, giving them a mental advantage, but as they were only two they moved with extra stealth and concentration, searching well ahead of themselves, pushing their eyes, ears and noses to their limits.

They reached a small clearing and Elmer hung back in the thicker bushes on the edge of it. He had decided they would wait here. His massive head stayed motionless and pointing forwards, nose twitching, ears turning slowly, and eyes looking for any sort of movement, his concentration was all consuming; whatever was out there he would let it come to them. The forest opening was about thirty strides across, Elmer was hoping this short distance would give them some time to assess the approaching danger and decide on their actions.

The intruder was becoming uneasy now and her youngsters, though quite large, were noticeably worried. She was pondering her present situation, deciding on her next move, when a familiar scent was caught on the breeze. Moving as quietly as possible she was about to turn back the way they had just come, but something stopped her. Another pair of wolf eyes was watching from the far side of the small clearing before her.

The owner of those eyes, Freya, emerged from the undergrowth in a low stalking stance, teeth bared, and gaze fixed on the intruders; she meant business. The trespassers stood their ground, the female had two big yearlings with her, and although much less experienced, their size and strength made them much more than a match for any one female. The intruder stared back hard at Freya, baring her own teeth and growling deeply, while her offspring hastily scanned the clearing and surrounding woods for any sign of others, they were getting even more uneasy.

All the interlopers eyes focused at once on the huge, powerful black wolf that was rushing at them from the other side of the clearing. The inexperienced youngsters panicked immediately and took off back the way they had come. Their mother was left alone now, and although a high status wolf herself, quickly thought better of standing her ground. She turned and ran too. Fight had rapidly turned to flight.

Speed was on Freya's side, she flew past Elmer and closed quickly on the larger, slower female. Realising she was unable to outrun her pursuers and not wanting to be tripped and attacked from behind the intruder turned to face them. She was the breeding female of a powerful pack and found it hard to be submissive to any other wolf except her own partner, but she was submissive now, her life might well depend on it. Often it was a packs dominant wolves that were killed in these situations as they would not back down, but her innate response of self preservation took over.

Freya wanted to kill this wolf or at least teach her a life threatening lesson but was body checked aside by Elmer before she could attack. Freya backed off, giving her mate some room. The lone female got as low as she could as Elmer approached, lowering her head to one side and licking her lips in an appeasement gesture, all the time emitting submissive whines, something she had not done for many years but still seemed to come naturally to her.

Elmer stood to his full height, showing his full weaponry and emphasising his great size and strength, he was almost twice as big as her. The lone female found herself becoming even more like a submissive, younger wolf before him, hoping to ward of a serious attack. Elmer's posture, teeth baring, and chorus of deep meaningful growls left her in no doubt of his power and the damage, or worse, that he could do to her. She could fight and no doubt cause some serious harm herself, but would probably not survive.

Intruding single wolves were often mortally wounded or killed by resident wolf packs, but after a prolonged show of submissive behaviour from the female and more serious posturing from Elmer, the final result seemed unclear. Freya was getting frustrated and rushed in, delivering a lightning quick bite to intruders rear, something to remember her by. The trespasser protested with meek signs of aggression, but they were intermingled with stronger signs of submission; in fear of something much worse.

As far as Freya was concerned their actions towards this intruder were nowhere near strong enough, but Elmer had made his decision. Standing tall and still growling, he allowed the lone wolf to get slowly to her feet. Keeping her body profile flat and low she slunk quickly away. Elmer hoped his actions would instil some sort of respect in this neighbour. Freya thought she would be back with others some day.

The recently killed deer fed them well for the next few days and they stayed close to it, Freya chasing off the ravens and other feathered scavengers when they dared to come down. Elmer ate, slept and often went off alone to patrol and mark their land; he was being extra vigilant.

Elmer thought often about their territory. It was not a big area but held enough prey for them. The river, with some low banks, provided easy access to water, and also attracted thirsty animals, it served too as a good boundary. The woodland was dense and healthy and the mountains on the opposite side from the river were also another natural barrier. Two other much larger packs bounded his land, and after recent events they were more often on his mind.

Freya too had been paying much more interest to their land recently, especially when near the river, innate thoughts were telling her she would need a good source of water close to her new den.

This would be her first time at motherhood and she carried only three pups, Mother Nature perhaps restricting the size of her litter for their territory and the amount of prey in it was not large. Freya knew the importance of what she had to do. Having a family, growing the pack, and passing on their genes was the goal of all adult wolves, she wanted to succeed and already she could feel the changes taking place within her. Soon, she would be unable to hunt so effectively, but she worried not with Elmer by her side.

CHAPTER 3

THE DENSITE

Freya had been paying a few visits to the large old tumble down oak that she now stood before, nosing around its exposed root system and searching the surrounding area. The great tree had come down years before in a storm to remember, and for a while now she had been thinking its spacious, partly exposed roots, might make a good place for her first den site. She would have to do a bit of digging though, to lengthen and deepen the tunnels that were already there, to afford more protection for her and the pups. The river was close by, with a shallow easy flowing stretch a short trot downstream, this should be safe for her young pups to explore. She thought again that it had promise. Freya made up her mind that this would be the location of her first den site, and she would start work on it today.

Elmer knew what was on Freya's mind as she disappeared into the dark hole below the fallen giant. Paw sized clods of dirt began flying out of the entrance. Elmer thought he should help her, like he did with the excavation of dens in his own birth pack, but something told him Freya wanted to do this herself. This was her first den and their pack was only the two of them, so he left her to it, and went off to remark their territory, if he was lucky he might also bring back some food for his partner. Elmer gave no real thought to the positioning of the den, this was Freya's decision, but he would always be there to defend it and his family, with his life if need be, for that was his way. Elmer turned and trotted happily off, leaving Freya to her work.

The big black wolf moved easily, his body flowing freely as he trotted to the regular marking spots near the boundaries of their land. He would leave his mark every few hundred yards as he made his way, each time lifting his leg as high as possible in a mission to get his urine mark elevated, allowing the smell of it to be carried further and more easily on the breeze. After urinating he almost always scraped the ground up with powerful backward swipes of all four paws.

He quickly came upon the familiar old tree stump, it was wider than he was long, one that he regularly marked on. Elmer jumped effortlessly up on top of it, marking it on the top rather than the side; height was everything. This remnant of a once immense oak was on the very edge of his territory, and served well as an obvious marker to all. Beyond it was a strip of land that had no owner, and past that you reached the neighbouring packs land. He had not ventured there yet.

Occasionally while travelling Elmer would find himself drawn to a particular tree. He would wait at the bottom of it looking up for a second before standing up on his back legs to reach up as high as he could with his front paws, then scratch the bark vigorously. Another visual sign of his size he thought, but it also felt good to him, it honed his claws. This high tree scratching behaviour was not so common for a wolf, but when young and impressionable Elmer had watched a particularly large and powerful bear carrying this same behaviour out, he knew that bear to be very dominant, and it had made some sort of lasting impression upon him.

When Elmer wanted to defecate he would find suitable places to do this too, often backing up onto a small bush or climbing on top off a tree stump to leave his sign higher up. Defecation also carried other messages within it, glands on either side of his anus would deposit story telling pheromones on his faeces as it emerged. Other times Elmer would just roll vigorously on the ground to spread his scent around, employing the pheromone producing glands on the side of his head, along his back and near the base of his tail.

Back at the new den site Freya was digging away feverishly and would soon have to reverse out of the tunnel to spread the spoil about. She emerged tail first into the daylight, squinting hard as her eyes adjusted to the stronger light. Straight away she set about scattering the large pile of newly dug earth from around the entrance with swift backward swipes of her paws, it did not take her long.

It was a hot day. The work and her present condition were having an effect on her, thoughts of a visit to the river for a wash, drink and a cooling lay down in the shallows, forced their way into her mind.

The water was clear and icy cold, it's source coming from the nearby mountains, so much so that she couldn't stay in it for too long. Like most wolves, water held no fear for Freya, when hunting she had often followed prey into the water. She was not so quick though to follow large, taller prey, into deep water. When with her birth pack she had seen a young juvenile male take a crippling head kick from a big deer stag, the wolf disadvantaged by having to swim around the longer legged prey that could stand grounded and strong on the river bed.

Freya laid in the water, enjoying the rapid cooling of her body. A large male swan, the cob, eyed her up from the safety of the far side of the river, but he would not dare have a go at an adult wolf. The cob and his pen were searching the river and it's backwaters for this years nesting site, like the wolf, they too, would soon be bringing up a family.

The wolf stared back hard at the swan, a natural response to the assertive attitude coming from the successful breeding male. The cob became just a little worried by her gaze and decided to move on. Unseen, the swan's huge webbed feet paddled away furiously in the water below, and the pair surged majestically away, a small v-shaped wake trailing in the water from the chest of each departing bird.

Freya left the water and after a few steps stopped to shake the excess from her body. Large droplets flew into the air, the bright sun catching them and making them shine, while the dry ground around received a welcome soaking. Freya made sure not shake too hard though, for she had learnt that staying a little wet kept her cooler for longer. More comfortable and relaxed she headed back to the den site to resume her digging; she was an intense and driven wolf when she had to be and was putting these traits to good use with the preparation of her first family home.

She was only twenty yards from the den site when something stopped her dead. A large black bear was reversing clumsily out of her new den entrance, she hadn't smelt him earlier as he had been moving about downwind of her. The bear was too big to enter the den, and already knew that there were no cubs in it, had there been he might now have been trying to dig them out. Freya puzzled at how she had not known he was about, had she been too intense in her digging and relaxed her senses. Almost instantly, and despite the bears greater size, she made up her mind to teach this bear a lesson, one that would make him think twice about ever returning to her den. Freya knew she would have to be careful though, black bears were much smaller and not as dangerous as brown bears, but they were still a powerful foe for just one wolf.

The intruder had smelt the wolf returning and knew she was there but with his back still turned Freya rushed forwards and delivered two quick bites to his rear. The bear swung round, more startled than hurt, he wanted to see his attacker; only one wolf. He let out a powerful roar towards her, Freya could feel the force of it vibrating in the air and her ears. She stared hard at the bear, trying quickly to assess her adversary. He was a young bear, and hopefully inexperienced with dealing with wolves. Freya had no cubs to protect but this was already her den site and she had worked hard on it.

The bear could see plainly the intenseness in the eyes of this wolf before him, and the meaningfulness of her body language. A pack of wolves with pups to protect might kill a black bear at their den site, a bear might kill one of the wolves, but there were no pups, and she was alone. Perhaps he might teach her a lesson.

Freya was heavily pregnant but this didn't enter her mind as she circled the large beast. He had not run as she had hoped and the bear was now shuffling around quickly to face her. He stood up tall on his back legs and bellowed again, displaying his greater size and strength. The bear thought to rush forwards when he came back down, and was just about too, when he caught sight of a large black shape moving about in the background.

With a heavy thud he landed on his massive, well furred front paws, and immediately searched for the dark shape he had seen. A huge black wolf now stepped into the open ground before him, body stiff and bristling, mouth large and open, lips curling completely back to expose his full weaponry. Elmer meant business.

Elmer thought nothing of why he should be about to fight a large black bear over an unfinished den site, but just about protecting his partner and the pups within her. The bear was young and large but the hesitancy within him was now becoming apparent to Elmer. The odds had changed, there could be more wolves about and the bear was now having second thoughts.

Buoyed up by the arrival of her partner and taking advantage of the bears in-decision, Freya flew in and delivered another quick slash to the bears rear. This would have to be her only tactic as head on would be too dangerous; if he managed to make contact with her it would not end well. Elmer joined the fray.

The two wolves continually harassed the slowly retreating bear, growling as they circled, and darting in and out to deliver snatched bites. They caused little real physical damage to the bear's large body but much to his shrinking resolve. The bear lunged out with a little roar when he thought he might have a chance of swiping one of the wolves, knocking them off balance and giving him time to do some serious damage; but he never did.

After only a few minutes the bear had made up his mind to go. There was nothing here worth fighting over. Turning quickly around he powered away at a speed that surprised both wolves. They followed for a short distance, the bear turning once to roar his disapproval but moving hastily on.

Elmer and Freya swung around together and trotted back to the den site as though little had just happened. Neither of them had been injured in the fight and Freya was sure that the bear had been taught a lesson, they would not see him again she thought. No more work on the den was done that day, they spent it in the company of each other reaffirming their bonds with shows of mutual affection. Freya had always known that Elmer was a good choice for a mate and he thought likewise.

The next day Freya carried on digging while Elmer went off to patrol. Freya had already doubled the length of the main tunnel but still had more to do, she was in the den digging away when some soil fell in from the roof, it was not a lot and she easily and quickly moved it to the entrance. Freya thought nothing of it and carried on with her work.

Elmer had been gone most of the morning when he reappeared carrying a large hare in his formidable jaws. Without ceremony he dropped it at the entrance to the den, turned and trotted quickly off, his relaxed tail swishing slowly from side to side. Freya emerged and grabbed up the hare, apart from the mark of the killing bite it was untouched. She happily carried it to the relative shade of a near beech tree and settled down to eat.

Freya's partner had found a good spot, some of the meadows on the fringes of their woodland held many rabbits and larger hares; he returned twice to the den in the next few hours, each time depositing a plump rabbit near the den entrance and trotting almost jubilantly off.

This was Freya's first den site and she had been driven by her innate instinct in selecting and shaping the first home for her imminent pups. Normally a wolf mother would pick a second den site in case of later problems with her first choice, a place to go to if they had to abandon it, but Freya had not come across a suitable place and dismissed the urge within; she would have no problems she thought. Freya was happy with the way things were going and thought the den was almost ready.

Later that day, satisfied with the job she had done, Freya emerged from the den, picking up the two rabbits that Elmer had left earlier. This time she wasn't going to eat the rabbits but store them in a cache for later, food was not scarce at the moment but she would bury them anyway. The warmer weather would make them spoil quickly but they might come in useful when she was nursing her pups, unable to hunt.

Freya quickly covered the ground until a reasonable distance from the den site. She didn't want to bury the rabbits too close for fear of another finding them, and then being too near to her family. Elmer appeared from nowhere, rubbing himself against his partner as he passed and making a mental note of where Freya was burying the food. He trotted on towards the den site leaving Freya to finish her task, if he was quick, he could have a look in the den on his own.

It was surprisingly cool in the bowels of the den, the tunnel went down and then back up to a small chamber at the back that would be roomy but not too big for a mother and pups. He could see why Freya had picked this spot. The ground was firm enough but not hard, easy digging he thought, making use of the natural space that was already beneath the old fallen oak, the trees roots should also add some strength to the den roof, and the river, a source of water, was only a short distance away. Elmer thought she had done well. It was his first den site too and he would do his utmost to keep them all safe. Freya returned as Elmer was leaving the den, she gave him a look that told him this was her place for now, and he trotted happily off.

The den finished, Freya could feel her time coming, but it wouldn't be today. She would stay close to the den site for the next few days, heading into it to stay when the time was right. Elmer would split his days between hunting, marking their territory and being around the den. Once Freya entered into the den to give birth and raise their pups he would have to work harder, something that worried him not. He was satisfying his urge to breed and have a family of his own. It felt good.

CHAPTER 4

LIFE IS PRECIOUS

The first pup came easily into the world. It was a female. Freya looked down in awe at the tiny bundle wriggling and squealing before her and for just a split second wondered what to do.

Her innate instincts quickly took over. She licked and gently nudged the wet, blood covered tiny body with her nose, becoming reassured by the many tiny sounds coming from it. Freya nipped the birth sac with her front teeth, tearing it some more, then pulled it away from around her pup and ate it, she would do this for all her newborns; it would keep the den clear and provide her with some valuable extra nourishment. Next Freya licked the pup all over to clean her. Further constant licking to the pup's genital area encouraged the pup to perform her first little elimination, and mum consumed this too. Freya would eat all of the pup's excrement while they were in the den, to keep it clean and safe for all of them; by three weeks old the pups would all be able to reach and eliminate outside, around the den entrance.

The tiny pup instinctively gravitated towards the warmth of her mother's body, Freya's licking to clean and stimulate her had done its job, but the little body had got cold. Blind and death the little pup nestled in.

Outside Elmer's keen senses told him of the emergence of life below ground and a wave of excitement swept through his body, making him howl and squeal like a pup himself. He flung himself on his back and wriggled violently sending clouds of dust high into the air, then jumped up and sprinted from one point to another in a show of shear joy. Elmer wanted to go in and take a closer look but fought of the urge for now, Freya still had a lot more to do.

Elmer calmed himself and took up a laying position in front of the den entrance, slumping his huge, heavy head down on massive, outstretched front paws. Occasionally, when he thought something new was going on, his head would lift back up and start nodding slightly from side to side, the ears on top swivelling around, trying to work out better what was taking place below the ground.

The first pup became disgruntled and whined at the movement of mum as she shuffled around to find the most comfortable position, preparing for the next imminent arrival. The second pup, another female, came a little less easily into the world, for she was quite a bit bigger. This birth took almost twice as long as the first, but soon the comforting sounds of another healthy new pup filled the den. Freya's innate instincts to mother kicked in again, she cleaned and stimulated her little treasure, then watched with the love of a new mother as the squealing pup made its way clumsily to the sanctuary of her warm body, joining her much smaller sister.

Freya knew there was one more pup still inside her, but something told her this one would be a while coming. She settled down as best she could, curling herself protectively around her new charges, responding to any of their squeals and moans with reassuring gentle licks and nudges, waiting for the waves of pain that would tell her to push the last pup out.

The pain was back and more intense now. She could easily put up with it but pondered why it was so much stronger. Freya soon got her answer. A massive and incredibly loud male pup now lay squirming at her feet. All newborn wolf pups were born dark in colour, taking on their adult colours later, but this one was jet black; just like Elmer.

Freya stared at the pup and wondered how such a large thing had come out of her, he looked twice the size of the biggest female pup. She removed his birth sack and cleaned him off, her attention quieting him down just a little, then gazed intently as the giant pup buried into her warm side, causing little murmurs of objection to erupt from his much smaller siblings. Freya imagined that this was just how Elmer might have started off in life and an inner pleasure washed over her.

Freya could relax a little now the hard work was over and she set about encouraging her new pups to find their first meal, gently nudging them in the right direction with her nose. After some blind shoving and paddling of uncontrolled limbs, all three found a teat, and their innate sucking reflex took over. The squealing, screaming and yelping stopped, and a silence broken only by an occasional contented moan took over.

Elmer could wait no longer. His excitement had risen every time he learnt of each birth below ground, especially with the birth of the third, noisiest pup. He plucked up some extra courage and moved slowly into the den. Elmer was looking for positive signs from Freya as he approached, and was instantly reassured as she gently rolled onto her side, revealing the feeding pups to him. It would normally be many days before a mother wolf would let another pack member into the den to see the pups, but the bond between this breeding pair could not have been greater.

There was not much room in the family area, dad gently sniffed and nudged his pups with a big wet nose. The big male pup reacted to the touch and let go of his teat, turning to investigate. Both his front paws fell uncontrolled onto his father's nose and with only the senses of touch and smell to guide him, he felt his way. Elmer stayed in this position for a while, positively loving the pup squirming around with no real purpose on his nose.

The other two pups continued feeding, emitting the odd squealing noise as if in recognition that something else was now near them. Elmer wanted to carry on experiencing the enjoyment with his new family but could sense his partners anxiousness to get her pups back together. He responded with a gentle flick of his head, pushing the big pup back towards Freya, then watched happily as his son latched back on to his teat and resumed suckling.

Elmer backed up slowly, pushing his head gently but firmly into the Freya's side as he passed, reversing out of the den an even happier wolf than when he came in.

Freya had been holed up in the den for two days now, nursing her pups, with Elmer just outside, always in close attendance. Elmer was getting the urge now to set off on a hunt, to get some food for his partner and himself, to provide for his new family. That urge quickly became stronger.

He decided it was time. Elmer's outward appearance quickly changed from one of captivated new father to that of a serious, powerful hunter. For the coming months feeding and protecting his pack, along with maintaining their territory, would be his main priorities in life. Plenty of good food for his partner would mean the best of health for his pups. These thoughts washed around in his mind as he moved off, but bothered him not. He welcomed the challenge.

Elmer did his job well, bringing a good supply of food to his mate. Deer, hare, rabbit and small rodents were in abundance, for it was also their time of year to reproduce. There were many young around and life for Elmer and his family was good. To make things easier for his partner he had been eating any prey he caught and then regurgitating it near the entrance to the den, so Freya could eat it quicker and get back to her pups. For the next few weeks the pups would live in a world of touch and smells with no sound or vision to go with it, totally reliant on their mother and father for food, warmth and safety. With Elmer provisioning and protecting them they all grew quickly.

It had been three weeks since the pups birth. The time had gone by with little to worry about except for Freya having to leave the den to see of an opportunist and rather rash red fox; he could easily have taken a pup given the chance and she could easily have caught and killed him, but after a short intense chase she had returned to her unguarded pups.

The pups eyes and ears were open now. They could walk around, if a little uncoordinated, and drawn by the light and sounds that came from the outside would often head towards the den entrance, always under the spell of their instinctive urge to explore. When they did get to the entrance they would stand there for a few seconds, squinting heavily while their new eyes adjusted to the brighter light. The pups noses had been working from day one, but now able to see and hear, they could start to associate physical things to the smells that previously had no real meaning to them. This onslaught of new experiences was relished by the bolder black pup, and he actively sort things out, his smaller sisters were just a little less enthusiastic.

Sometimes when the pups ventured to the den entrance Elmer would be there. He would take any opportunity to socialise with his pups and they never seemed wary of him, it was as though they already knew who this powerful and caring wolf was, and they always tried to engage with him.

Elmer loved being around his pups, but Freya always kept a motherly eye on things, when she thought they had been away from her long enough she would pick them up gently by the scruff and deposit them back in the den. It seemed to her that she was more often having to travel further to retrieve the big black pup. She would have to keep an extra eye on him.

The large pup was by far the boldest of the bunch, but despite his greater size and strength Freya sometimes witnessed him giving way to his sisters when feeding, this might change as he got older but the behaviour reminded her of Elmer's ways. The smallest pup was often finding herself pushed aside by her larger sister when feeding or when something of interest like mum and dad were about. Freya could see what was going on but didn't intervene unless things got out of control, this was normal behaviour among wolves and part of the learning process and socialisation in wolf society.

Solid food was now becoming of interest to the pups. Investigating the regurgitated offerings brought back by Elmer was now a regular occurrence, for now though, it was more about experimenting with tastes and textures, but they would soon be consuming solid food in earnest, as well as taking mother's milk.

The weather, even though summer had arrived, had been challenging. Unseasonable heavy rain had been falling for several days now, and the ground around was much wetter than normal for this time of year. The river was running much higher than usual, fuelled by the excess water entering the river upstream from the mountains and the extra run off from the waterlogged land. The roar of the swollen river was obvious yet still unknown to the pups, it scared them sometimes. Freya didn't worry about it, she had heard such before and knew what it was, but she wouldn't ignore her anxious pups, she released calming pheromones from glands on her body, smells that the pups would recognize and settle down to.

Four weeks had passed since the birth of the pups and they regularly made their way to the den entrance to eliminate, look out, listen to, and smell the world outside. If Elmer was in residence at the den area he would quickly become excited and look to interact with the pups, they would always react with joy just as feverish as his own and intense play around the den entrance would follow.

Freya had spent nearly all her time these four weeks with the pups. Recently she had wanted to get out and take part in some hunting but found that after leaving the pups to join Elmer on a hunt she would only travel a short distance then turn and sprint back to them. These were her first pups and she didn't like leaving them yet. Elmer knew how Freya felt, their pups were just as precious to him as well, he worked extra hard to keep his family well fed, so that Freya would not have to hunt.

The pups were now taking real interest in the regurgitated food brought in by Elmer. It was still early days as far as eating fresh meat was concerned, it was still a bit hard for them to digest, but a little fight would sometimes break out as each tried to claim a little piece for themselves. Already the pups had become adept at soliciting food from their father, when Elmer did put in an appearance they would run towards him, squealing and whining, then push their little heads up under his chin, licking and nudging his mouth, stimulating him to regurgitate his latest meal. Like most wolf pup fathers Elmer found it almost impossible not to react to his pups advances, it was as though this reaction was out of his control, and a pile of fresh steaming meat was almost always the result. Suckling from Freya decreased in regularity and length of time as more solid food was being taken, but it still took place. All the pups, even the smallest, could now suckle easily with mum standing up.

Play took up much of the pup's time, games of chase and pounce, wrestling, ambushing and annoying mum and dad. Now the pups were stronger Elmer made a point of coming more often into the den site, the pups always left whatever they were doing to come over and interact with their father, the over exuberant black pup often receiving a gentle clout from one of his huge paws to calm him down, but the effect never seemed to last long though. Sometimes Elmer would go out of his way to play with the little female, often to the annoyance of the other two, but he would ignore their whining and continue playing with her, he didn't want her, or himself, to lose out.

Elmer loved playing with his pups, it made him feel like one himself. Often he would start proceedings by carrying out a play bow to encourage it; sinking down on his front paws with his rear end up in the air and staring intently with a play face, he would then bounce towards them with quick little jumps keeping his body rigid in the same position. The result was always the same, any pups present would rush at him to play.

Another week went quickly by, the weather remained unseasonably wet, yet was still unable to dampen the young families feelings. All the pups were getting stronger and bolder, regularly leaving the den entrance now to explore the immediate area around it, the large black one venturing much further away than the others. Both Elmer and Freya were well aware of the big pup's ways and often found themselves having to go and look for him when it was time to sleep in the den.

Today, the big pup had decided to investigate the loud noise he had been hearing since his ears first opened. Lately it had been much louder and it drew the bold youngsters attention like a magnet. He let his ears lead him, the draw of the familiar yet unknown sound pulling him quickly away, much further than his little legs and enthusiasm had previously ever taken him. The big pup knew that he was too far from his mother and the den but he was close, so he carried on.

The grass was getting higher, taller than him, but he barged his way through it. The greenery started turning into reeds now, stiffer and harder to get through, posing some sort of an obstacle, so he pushed on harder; that loud noise was really close now. Movement suddenly became easier as he burst out onto a small, stony spit of land, that jutted out very slightly into the swollen, fast moving water.

This was the first time he had seen the river and he now knew that this was the rumbling that he had been hearing since his ears had first opened. He looked on with a pups inquisitiveness at this seemingly great power before him. The bright sunlight was reflecting of the water, dancing around and attracting him closer. Standing as tall as he could he dabbed at the rushing water just below him with one of his front paws, all the time keeping his other paws planted firmly on the ground. He was somehow captivated by the sparkly, fast moving water, and didn't see the bushy log being driven hard and fast down the river towards him.

As the piece of broken tree flew by, one of it's branches reached out like a tentacle and caught hold of him, making him squeal in surprise, before dragging him off his feet and into the rushing water. It was freezing. The sudden shock made the pup suck in air quickly. The river, normally easy flowing and placid, was fast and powerful. Instantly scared he was swept away.

Tiny webbed paws instinctively paddled away furiously but had little effect. He managed to grab the odd breath through the bubbling water but sometimes not only air was taken in, it made him splutter heavily. The terrified pup cried out as loud as his little lungs allowed but the noise from the rushing water was too great; none could hear him.

Luck was maybe on his side, downstream the river bent quickly to the right and the current pushed him into some shallower, slower moving water. He was still unable to touch the bottom but something told him to make for the near bank, summoning up some extra strength he paddled ferociously.

Elmer was returning from a hunting trip, his tail wagging slowly from side to side, a hare clamped firmly between his considerable jaws. It was the first whole animal he would be bringing to the pups since their birth and he was interested to see their reaction to it. He was approaching the shallow part of the river not far from the den and heard a sound that drew his attention.

A loud repetitive beating noise filled the air. Elmer could hear the loud slaps above the drone of this less noisy stretch of river and he knew what it was. A swan was attacking something. Loud beating noises made by the huge wings of the cob swan striking the water as he ran furiously across the top of the water to do battle, filled the air.

The pup was truly fighting for his life now, out of his depth, freezing cold, and running on his last reserves of energy. He was being pushed repeatedly under the water by a huge, angry bird. The swan was the local breeding territorial male, he regularly patrolled this part of the river to let any others of his kind know it belonged to him. Normally he would swim up and down but the rough water of late didn't allow this so he would let the current push him down river

31

then take off and fly back up it to start again. He meant to drown the small intruder.

The little pup tried in vain to fight back, his small needle teeth managing to bite the enraged swans leg, but nothing was felt as its wrath built further.

An inquisitive Elmer had reached the bank of the river about twenty paces from the battling swan, he strained his eyes to try and see the target of the birds fury. Elmer couldn't make out what the swan was trying to hold under the water but instantly recognized the high pitched cries that rippled across the top of the water and surged into his ears.

Elmer's reaction was reflexive, dropping his hare and launching into the river. The water was cold but Elmer didn't take any notice of it at all as he rushed towards the enemy. The tall, powerful wolf could stand easily in the two feet of rushing water, the current was strong but he was stronger, Elmer quickly covered the ground.

The swan, blinkered by his rage, didn't see the adult wolf bearing down on him, and carried on his attack. Just seconds later he saw him, a totally focused killer closing quickly. Momentarily, the swan froze rigid with fear, a second later, and the cob forced himself to snap out of it. Webbed feet paddled furiously as he turned to try and make his escape, but he had left it far too late. It took the big swan precious seconds to try and get his heavy wings and body moving, he paid the ultimate price.

Elmer grabbed the flapping swan by the head and killed him instantly with one bone crushing bite. With no further thought for the swan he dropped it and scanned the rough water for his pup.

The swift current had taken the little body quickly downstream, Elmer tore off after him. The water quickly got deeper and Elmer had to swim hard, to try and catch him up. The sight of one of his pups, only a short distance away, struggling to stay alive, drove him on.

The big wolfs powerful, determined strokes, brought him close to his son, but both were still being swept along at the mercy of the river. Elmer wrestled with the water, trying to get near as his silent, limp pup bobbed about around him.

Spluttering himself now and taking in large mouthfuls of water he tried to reach out, extending his neck as far as he could to grab him. Elmer repeatedly lunged out, each time becoming more fraught as the water moved his pup away. He wouldn't give up. Eventually he managed to grab just one of his pups ears. Elmer turned his back on the current, to shield the pup and give him a chance to get a better grip. Risking all he pulled the little body quickly upwards, out of the water, towards him, then let go and made a lightning quick grab for his body. Success. He now held his pup more safely, by his middle.

It took all of Elmer's considerable strength to battle across the current, all of the time taking care to try and keep his pups head out of the water. Slowly but surely he reached the bank. Elmer dragged himself up the steep riverside, the lifeless pup in his jaws. The river had taken them several hundred yards downstream. Without stopping to shake the water from his body, or checking on his son, he summoned up more energy and sprinted back to the den.

A distressed Freya had already started barking for her missing pup, Elmer could hear the pangs of anxiousness within her as he closed. Freya knew instinctively something was very wrong when Elmer appeared soaking wet and moving fast, her missing pup limp in his jaws. He laid the pup quickly but gently on the ground at Freya's feet and backed away. She immediately started licking and nosing him, there was no reaction. She carried on pushing and pulling the little body with even more vigour, in a bid to wake him. Little whines started coming from her now as she feared the worse. Elmer stood still, quiet and intense, watching her.

The other two pups had come over now and knowing that something serious was taking place they stood silently beside their dripping wet father. Freya was getting frantic now in her attempts to wake her son until finally, a small whimper escaped from the bedraggled little body. Elmer ears stood on end as he heard it and he sank down on all fours, watching almost unbelieving as the big pup came back to life; he was truly a fighter.

Totally exhausted, soaked and freezing, the pup whined and cried loudly as Freya comforted him with gentle, reassuring licks and nudges. The other pups joined in too now, adding their own bodily warmth to their freezing brothers and nestling into him. Elmer rose back to his feet and moved a few feet away before finally shaking the water from his body.

The whole event had been a truly scary experience for the big pup, one that he would never forget. From now on he would carry a true respect for the river, and a lifelong hatred of swans.

Further down the river a swan was sat on her nest, brooding this years clutch of eggs. The huge platform nest of twigs, leaves and other plant stems, was built amongst a raft of floating vegetation in the centre of a calmer and more secluded backwater. The pen had not seen her mate all day, and was keeping a vigil for his safe return. As she looked on the flattened and lifeless body of a swan appeared on the main river, floating quickly and silently by.

The mother swan left her nest, flopping hurriedly into the water. She paddled furiously out of the calm backwater into the fast flowing river, to catch up to his body, to make sure what she really already knew. She couldn't stay with him for long, the nest would be hard to get back too.

His death would be a great loss to her for he was supposed to be her mate for life. Head hung low she made her way slowly back, the river was too rough for her to take off and fly back, she stayed tight to the bank where the water was a little easier.

Tired and subdued she got back to her nest and it's six eggs. With a couple of hops and a few flaps of her giant wings, she got back up on it. Sitting down she moved her backside around in circles, getting comfortable on her clutch. Settled back down her thoughts turned to her lost partner and the eggs beneath her. Just like many other single swans her life had now become much harder, but she could, and would, bring up her family alone.

CHAPTER 5

WATER, LIFE GIVER AND LIFE TAKER

The river was still running high, it's power was obvious to all the family by the roar it made, especially to the pups when underground in their home, the earth seemed to move with it. Elmer had never seen it so.

Nearly six weeks old the pups spent much of the daytime exploring the area around the den site, the nervous little female still not straying too far from the safety of the den.

It was evening when the big pup came trotting back into the den area, looking immensely pleased with himself, a small piece of rabbit hide in his jaws. Elmer thought his son behaved like he was bringing a whole deer to his hungry family and an inner warmth came over him.

The pup continually tossed the hide into the air, looking for signs of interest from the rest of his family. The large female pup came rushing over and tried to grab the hide from him, but he was ready for her, this was what he had been waiting for. He scooted off with his prize, one eye watching to see if he was being followed. For the next few minutes he strutted around the den site showing of his tiny prize, poking it teasingly into the faces of his sisters and Father, inviting someone to try and take it off him.

Freya appeared, the light was beginning to fade and she thought it was time for her pups to retreat to the den. She gave the big boy a look which said it all. He reluctantly dropped his little prize and head down, trotted towards the den entrance. The small female saw her chance and ran past him, grabbing up the hide with a triumphant pose and tossing it aloft, catching it several times before leaving it where it fell. The two female pups filed in behind their sulking big brother.

Tonight the noise of the river was louder than ever. Several days of heavy rain had swollen it beyond compare and the pups huddled together tighter than normal into their mothers body. Freya could feel their anxiousness and responded as usual by releasing calming pheromones from glands on her body, to help settle them down. Elmer lay outside, sheltering under a broad leaved oak, not too far away.

The storm was right overhead. Fingers of lightning shot across the dark sky, followed almost instantly by deep, rumbling rolls of thunder that seemed to make the air itself vibrate. Howling winds were accompanied by long, heavy rain showers, that drove down vertically into the ground, breaking it apart. The noise and power of the weather outside didn't allow the pups to relax, none of them slept, they were all on edge.

Freya and her pups all sprung to their feet as one, an ear splitting sound, loud and drawn out, sliced through the air. A once mighty oak, over sixty feet tall, had been found by a bolt of lightning as it searched out a way to the ground. The excess water held in the old trees deeply furrowed bark had given the electricity an easier way to the ground. The power of the strike would be the final nail in the great trees coffin, tonight it would lose a century long battle to stay upright on the bank of the river. Nearly six hundred years old, and the home for a myriad of woodland creatures, the leviathan crashed down into the river. It's falling would have far reaching effect.

The river was at its most powerful but it could not dislodge the massive oaks trunk. It now stretched out across the top of the water, spanning it's width easily, wedged firmly between the two opposite banks. The trees huge stem was acting like a dam, funnelling large amounts of water from the top of the river along its length and over the banks, into the surrounding land. The escaping water, fuelled constantly by the swollen river behind it, quickly grew and surged outwards. At it's head fingers of water were searching out any low land or hole before it, filling them quickly before moving unstoppably on. The den was in its path.

After hearing the loud crack Freya had gone out into the darkness to investigate, leaving her worried pups in the safety of the den. She had gone only a few hundred yards when a long sustained crack of lightning shot across the sky, illuminating the area in front of her. It looked different. The ground was somehow reflecting the light, just like water did. Freya immediately started to worry. The small wave of advancing water was clear to her now, in seconds it was at her feet. She turned back towards the den and stood frozen for just a moment, as things sunk in. The water was advancing at different points, following the lay of the land, and an arm of it was already well ahead of Freya, passing over the roof of the den. She exploded off, back towards her family.

The tree roots above the roof of the den afforded good protection from something trying to dig it's way in, but the searching fingers of water made their way easily between them. Large drops of water started to fall on the huddling pups little bodies and all three rose quickly to their feet. Before any of them could make a move the trickles turned to a gush, torrents of water and mud burst it's way in.

Together, the pups scrambled for the entrance, but the roof of the den tunnel ahead of them fell in with a deafening, heavy thud. A gush of air shot up the up the tunnel into their faces, stopping them dead; it was completely blocked. The pups were now trapped in a small length of the den tunnel with water pouring in through the mud from both ends, not a sign of a way out anywhere. Their sanctuary and place of safety, had now become something else.

The big black pup moved first. He jumped forwards and started to dig furiously at the large pile of sodden earth between him and the entrance; the way out was always this way. His sisters sat huddled together behind him in the wet, muddy tunnel, crying and frightened, watching as their brother dug with all the strength his little body could muster.

Freya arrived back at the den in seconds but it had already collapsed. She scanned the area around quickly but there was no sign of any pups, already she knew they were still inside. Freya dashed right up to the broken down den entrance, placing one ear to the ground and listening as best the weather allowed her. She could hear the digging pup inside. Without thought she started digging towards the noise. There was a huge pile of soil between them. Mother and son both dug ferociously.

Elmer had not been far away, and he reached the den just after Freya to see her already digging. She didn't even stop to look at him. He rushed down and took his place beside her, his great strength making an instant impact as huge pawfuls of mud flew behind him.

The water kept coming, the soil that they were digging out turned to heavy wet mud beneath them, making it harder to clear away. Elmer moved back behind Freya to throw the sticky black stuff further back, his paws beginning to bleed. Freya began to whimper. Elmer growled deeply at the mud and burrowed even harder.

The roof of the den that still stood above the pups was getting wetter and heavier, inside the two females now began whimpering and crying in earnest. The big pup growled just like his mighty father outside, and carried on digging.

They were not far away from each other now, the male pup could sense it, but then the world fell in on him. Heavy wet mud and a cascade of water crashed down on the pups as the last bit of the den roof caved in, the heavy, gooey mud, flattening and pinning all three to the tunnel floor.

The big pup laid there for a second, struggling to breath under the weight on top of him, but he didn't want to die. Summoning all the remaining strength within him he pushed upwards with all his legs at the same time. There was a little movement to start with, he could feel the mud starting to lose it's grip on him, a few more seconds, and he burst out of his sticky prison. Pushing up through the wet mud with his little black nose he was met by a much bigger nose surging down through it. He cried and licked the caked on mud from the tip of his fathers nose with his raspy little tongue, and for a second time Elmer dragged the big pup from almost certain death.

Elmer scooped him up and carried him several yards from the den to some slightly higher and safer ground, Freya watched him as he passed her, but didn't move from her position. Elmer laid him down gently under a large oak. He quickly looked over the shaking and trembling little body, giving him some quick soft licks and reassuring nudges before returning to dig beside Freya. Cold, wet, dazed and bewildered, the pup cried almost silently, and waited.

Freya could smell the other pups and forced her nose down through the mud and water below her. She felt one of them and struggled frantically, moving her open mouth around in a bid to get a grip on her little body, turning her head one way then the other, until sure she had her. She pulled firmly but slowly. There was a loud popping sound as she freed the larger female pup from the sucking grip of the mud and water. Freya lifted the unmoving pup up and trotted quickly to the other one. She had only recently seen the lifeless body of their big pup come back to life, and she thought the same would happen with her. She laid the motionless pup next to her big brother, then set about vigorously nudging and licking her.

Nothing happened. The little body didn't move. She tried again and again, her despair showing itself as she whined deeply. The male pup tried to crawl towards her but Freya stopped him, leaving the pup she was working on to quickly nose and reassure him. She backed up, looked longingly at her still lifeless pup, then returned to dig for the last one. As she left the big pup rolled over onto his smaller sister and wrapped his body around her, trying to warm her; small whimpers and cries came from him as he nudged and licked her constantly.

Elmer and Freya were both digging with controlled rage now as they searched for their third pup, the smallest and weakest; how dare the river take her. It was not much longer before they found her, but Freya knew it had already been too long. Elmer pulled the smallest pup out by her soaked, muddy scruff and carried the crumpled body to the others. Freya, head bowed, followed on, sure in the knowledge that she had already lost two of her precious pups.

Freya could not believe her eyes. The big pup was licking the face of the other female pup and she was licking him back, she was alive, and for a second Freya felt glad. Elmer laid the smallest pup down beside the other two and stepped away. All the family watched as Freya spent several minutes nudging, licking and rolling the smallest pup in a vain bid to revive her, but she already knew the outcome. The two surviving pups crawled over and laid on their dead sister letting out small whines and nudging her in a final attempt to warm and stimulate her, but as young as they were, they too, soon realised that this was the end.

It was his duty to protect his family and although Elmer could have done nothing about it he felt in some way responsible. He was glad that the two first pups had survived but was saddened greatly for the loss of the other one, the feelings within him seemed even stronger than when he had lost brothers and sisters from his own birth pack. He had loved their little pup a lot.

Elmer cast a saddened look towards Freya before padding over and picking the little pup up gently in his jaws. Freya and the two pups watched on as Elmer disappeared into the night. He would find a place to leave her.

Freya lay down with her pups, the relative shelter of the oak tree above them, and they buried tightly into her side. She spent the next few minutes nudging and licking them, reassuring them, making sure they were warm and well.

It was some time before Elmer returned. He buried his head into Freya's side, then took big sniffs of both his surviving pups, soaking up their smells. Mother and Father joined together in trying to make sure their two remaining pups felt safe and protected.

The rain had stopped. It was time to go. Elmer picked up the big pup by his scruff and looked towards Freya. She picked up the other pup, and with them both hanging limp from their jaws they set off through the water logged land. They wanted to get out of this place. The pups were probably big enough now to follow them but both felt the need to carry them for a while, to make sure they were safe. Elmer followed Freya, where they went now would be Freya's decision. She would try to find somewhere safe for her little family.

After a couple of hours the family stopped for a time to rest under a raggedy old beech tree. Freya stayed with the pups and Elmer went off alone, his head hung low. Just a few minutes later and a chorus of long mournful howls filled the night air. Elmer carried on his vigil until it was almost light, Freya and the pups listening on quietly. Freya felt like joining her partner in his howling but wanted to try and stay quiet and calm with her still worried charges beside her. The pups had heard their father howling before but even they could sense the difference in his howls that night. He was missing the little one.

CHAPTER 6

FAMILY FIRST

Well before her pups were born Freya had been scouting out good future homesites for her family to occupy, but she had not been expecting to have to use one so early in the pups lives. A dense clump of beech trees with thick ground cover had looked good to her in those times and she had kept it's whereabouts in her mental list of suitable sites for the future. It was daylight and Elmer had returned from his lone howling, she took the lead and headed there, her small family in tow.

This had been Freya's first litter and she would learn from her mistakes. She should have had a second den site ready to move into in case of a problems with her first but now the worst had happened and the pups were being taken to a temporary, less safe site. At just six weeks old the pups should have been spending a few more weeks in the safety of a proper den. Freya felt that maybe it was because of her actions that they now headed for this more vulnerable place. Her thoughts went back to the little female pup they had lost, had her choice of den site been to blame? Next time she would not chose a den site so low lying and close to the water.

They reached the new homesite area. Elmer and Freya had moved slower than normal at times to allow the pups to walk some of the way. The site was a large clump of beech trees about 150 feet across, in the middle of a larger surrounding forest of oak, birch and more beech. The cover on the forest floor and in the homesite was dense and high. Freya would have to work hard to make tracks into it for her pups, she would make sure it was as safe as possible for them.

The sun had come out with a vengeance and it felt like summer had returned. The pups set about jumping all over their father. Elmer happily returned their advances but there wasn't quite his usual intense reactions.

Freya got to work. All the family seemed to know that she wanted to do this on her own and they left her to it. The inquisitive big pup couldn't stay away completely from the work in progress though, often he would amble over to take a sneaky look, moving on when Freya spied him and gave one of her looks.

The mother wolf spent much of the day preparing the site, clearing two small paths through the dense scrub into the centre of the clump, at the end of these she flattened an area for the family to lay in. While Freya toiled away Elmer played again with his son and daughter, this time with a little more enthusiasm; they had lost one pup but there were still two more to bring up.

It was early evening. Freya cast her eyes slowly over what she had done and happy with the outcome trotted over to take her place beside a snoozing Elmer and pups. Elmer lifted his huge head on Freya's approach and she lowered herself almost to his height before nuzzling into the side of his face, then toppling into his side.

Her arrival woke the worn out pups from their slumber just a few feet away, both jumped enthusiastically to their feet and rushed quickly over, not wanting to miss out on some family bonding. The big pup crashed onto his father while his sister fell less heavily into her mother. The male pup was already a fair weight but Elmer welcomed the closeness, and so did Freya. The new site was ready to use but they stayed were they were, enjoying the moment before drifting off. The next few days would be spent relaxing in and around their new homesite.

Play between the pups on their own was becoming more rough and tumble now as each started to test the other. Physically the big male pup was much stronger and he easily won the wrestling matches between them. Often, he would pin his much smaller sister down, only letting her up when he sensed the rage building up within her, he would then rush off with his angry sister in hot pursuit, snapping wildly at his back legs. Being much lighter and faster she would catch him easily, but couldn't trip him up yet. Sometimes he would let her roll him over, then burst up and chase her. They regularly played games of hide and seek, or ambushing each other. This sort of play would help with the development of their strength and hunting skills. Elmer always watched his pups intently, seeing likenesses in their behaviour that reminded him of Freya and himself, it made him happy.

It was their third day at the new site and the family lay together in a big pile outside the entrance. The weather was more like it should be for this time of year now. The morning sun sat low in the sky, already it had some power, warming their bodies with its rays when finding them. All seemed well. The birds morning chorus was ebbing away as the family lazily stretched their bodies out while still laying down.

The wolf father was listening to the high pitched moans of his pups as they yawned with wide open mouths when a sudden chorus of raucous warning calls were belted out by some nearby ravens. Elmer sprung instantly to his feet, scattering the startled pups on the ground and scanning the area quickly. Freya was just a second behind him.

One raven carried on it's crowing. The whole family now stood to attention, their heads pointing together in the direction that the big black bird somehow showed. Ears swivelled and noses twitched as the array of senses, big and small, scanned the the forest before them. Something was amiss.

He waited only a few seconds before purposefully heading off to investigate. Freya woofed a quiet warning before ushering the pups towards their temporary home. The big pup stopped in the entrance and turned around, scanning the forest with a seriousness to match his fathers, he already looked prepared to defend them. After some more prompting from Freya he eventually went in to lay with his sister. Freya turned to follow on after Elmer, then quickly changed her mind. Elmer looked back with a knowing gaze as she returned to watch over their pups.

Elmer moved slowly but deliberately forward, he could smell nothing on the breeze as it came from behind him. He moved with care. His keen eyesight picked out the movement of another large animal ahead of him, it also was moving slowly and purposefully like him, Elmer knew it was another of his kind. Straining his senses even further, he looked for some signs, trying to work out how many might be before him. He would have taken on any number of foe so close to his family, but he was soon sure that there was only one

43

intruder. Being in his own territory gave Elmer extra confidence and more importantly a mental edge over another. Moving slowly and deliberately forwards he made himself as tall as possible, to try and intimidate the trespasser. Coming to a halt Elmer stood solidly still, his huge head and body motionless, a look of intenseness etched into his face that should have scared any other single wolf; but not this one it seemed. A wolf as tall as himself stepped deliberately into the small clearing before him.

The other wolf, also a male, might have rivalled Elmer in size had he been in top condition, it was just a little encouraging that he wasn't. There was though, something familiar about this tall, skinny wolf before him. With still no scent to help him Elmer moved forwards again, to try and get a better look. The intruder stood his ground.

The sunlight was bright and right in Elmer's eyes, he screwed them up to try and help find some more detail, but none was forthcoming, he could though, make out the other wolf's outline, and the body language he was displaying. The trespassers tail was sitting horizontal behind him, with only the end of it moving very slowly from side to side, a definite communication that he was not sure of the present situation. The intruders other signs of relaxed ears and closed mouth were telling him that harm was probably not on his mind. He moved closer still.

Elmer was still not sure, he let the other wolf know this by keeping his own tail stiff and straight up, his body as tall as he could make it, and any movements tight and calculated. Closing in further he moved into shadow and not blinded by the sun any more was finally allowed to see clearly the wolf before him. Elmer visibly shrunk as he relaxed. His large bushy tail began swishing around madly as he trotted happily over to the other wolf. The newcomer's tail responded in kind as he stood still and waited for Elmer to reach him.

Elmer buried his head deep into his fathers side and both pushed against each other in a show of affection, they turned and stood eye to eye for a second, then both became loud and spirited in their greetings. Elmer held back some of his great strength, he wanted to become even more exuberant, like he did when he was in his fathers pack, but already he could sense his weakness, so he held back the urge, just a little.

As son played with father, like they did just months before, Elmer thought about why he was here. His father was alone, and Elmer knew he would never have left his mother if she was still alive. His actions of exuberance suddenly became tinged with ones of worry.

His fathers family had recently been displaced by a younger, stronger and much larger neighbouring pack. Months of territorial strife and minor skirmishes leading up to this time had been very intense and worrying for Elmer's parents, the long term stress resulting in no pups being born this year. In the final battle for their territory his mother had been killed, and father seriously injured, their remaining pack of six had dispersed and gone their own ways.

Forced to leave his dead partner and home behind his father had wandered alone in search of some kind of help with his grief, to find some companionship and maybe meet up with some of his own pack. Eventually he had come across the familiar scent of Elmer and his family. He recognized instantly the welcoming scent of his son, and had followed it.

Elmer's father had been badly injured in the fight for his family and their home, this had seriously affected his hunting capability and so he hadn't eaten for many days. At nearly ten years old his father had done well to keep his pack and territory protected for so long, but now, a weaker and much less confident wolf stood before his son.

Elmer would not turn him away, the thought had not even entered his mind, he was his father, the one that had taught him the things that made him a successful wolf today, he still held great respect and admiration for him; but what would Freya make of things. Exuberant greetings over, Elmer turned and started trotting slowly back towards his new home. He stopped and looked back over his shoulder, beckoning his father to follow him, only turning his head back to the path when his father started moving. It felt strange to Elmer that his once mighty father was now following him, like the roles had somehow been reversed. As he moved he thought again about his mother and the rest of his old family, and for a moment became inwardly saddened.

Freya emerged from the scrub as Elmer approached and was not reassured by his quietness, something told her things were not quite right. The pups rushed past her to greet their father but quickly stopped dead in their tracks as their gaze went past Elmer and fell on the approaching wolf behind him. Freya's behaviour changed immediately, her body sank down lower into an aggressive forwards pointing stance with fixed, staring eyes, not sure what was going on she was preparing to attack. The pups turned and ran back behind their mother, standing in silence they watched closely as things unfolded.

Elmer stopped and turned back towards his father. He trotted over and buried his head into his side. His father responded in kind, pushing back into Elmer, then flopping slowly onto his side, soliciting attention, an outward show of affection and submission. Freya relaxed slightly as she witnessed the obvious closeness and respect between the two males, but was still unsure. This new male was old, thin and carrying obvious injuries, but she somehow sensed that there was no malice in him.

The pups stayed where they were, watching as Freya moved cautiously forwards to meet Elmer's father. Freya could never be as welcoming as Elmer but was already sure of the bond between them, and she trusted her partners judgement. Maybe their pack had temporarily grown by one she thought, time would tell.

Elmer called the pups and both rushed over to be near him, they too trusted their father's ways unquestionably, he would never do anything to put them in jeopardy. Elmer's father, Orin, watched from a short distance, with eyes that were happier than they had been for many days. A wolf was not meant to spend long periods of time alone and he was truly happy to be with Elmer and his family. Freya though, still kept one of her eyes on Orin.

CHAPTER 7

ACCEPTANCE

The family had spent a couple of days getting used to having Orin around, no hunting had taken place, and Elmer was now getting a strong urge to do some. Orin could see the change in his son's behaviour, the heightened senses and outward look of expectancy, he knew what Elmer was thinking and prepared himself to accompany him; he may have been weaker than normal but still had great experience and an eagerness to use it, and he was hungry. Freya too, could see what was on Elmer's mind, easily picking up on her partners body language, but she would stay with the pups today.

Exuberant whines, howls and lots of excited barging became the order things as Elmer and his father readied to move off. The pups were a few metres away, and as normal couldn't control themselves, they had to join in, both having their own little moment, but still giving Orin a little room. Minutes later the madness subsided. Elmer done his final shake before moving off, his father happily bringing up the rear.

Elmer, as always, moved confidently through his forest. Orin watched him closely, impressed with the wolf his son had become: big, strong and courageous, these things his father had already known, but now he could also see the fairness and compassion within. They followed a well used woodland track in the hope of coming across some signs of prey, both scenting the air continually while moving, trying to distinguish the smell of possible quarry from the other forest odours that flooded in.

Today was to be one of those lucky days. It wasn't long before the track started to became heavy with the recent scent of wild boar. Boar were a favourite prey and Elmer knew they could not be far away. Orin knew too, and followed his sons lead. Leaving the hardly visible track they headed into the trees.

Wild boar travelled in extended family groups, mostly made up of sows with piglets and juveniles of varying ages. The larger and more dangerous adult male boar would come and go. The dominant males were more often about during the breeding times in late autumn, they were large, much more aggressive, and best left alone. As the wild boar clan moved about they turned over large areas of woodland with their noses in search of food, leaving obvious signs that they had been by, their powerful neck and shoulder muscles made light work of most things that got in their way.

These wild pigs spent much of their time grubbing about for acorns, bulbs and tubers, they were not fussy though, and really anything they came across that seemed edible would be eaten, including carrion. Wild boar were always high on Elmer's list of preferred prey, but extra care had to be taken when they had piglets to protect.

The loud snorting of digging adults and squealing piglets could be heard easily above the other woodland sounds. Elmer and Orin closed in. The boar family was an extended group of about twenty individuals, six piglets with their mother, a large Sow, with a mix of juveniles and young adults, the dominant Boar was nowhere to be seen.

Both hunters surveyed the scene, their predatory minds hard at work looking for any obvious target, one with injury, disease, or just old, but all that they could see seemed fit and healthy. Elmer decided he would take on one of the medium sized juveniles.

Orin laid down where he was and Elmer made his way slowly and steadily around the side of the family. He hadn't got far when 'Crack!' A large dried out twig snapped easily under his weight, the sharp, piercing noise announcing the presence of something to all nearby. For just a second Elmer was deeply aggravated by his mistake.

The advantage of surprise was now gone. Most of the boar's heads were up, scanning and sniffing the forest for danger, many of them letting out worried grunts. Elmer didn't waste any more time and rushed in. The dominant Sow and some of the sub-adults grunted a chorus of loud warnings as the perpetrators became clear, the piglets began squealing madly, bomb bursting off in all directions, to confuse, and to search out a hiding place.

The big Sow quickly assessed the situation and for a second thought to charge the incoming wolf, had the clan Boar been with her she certainly would have done, but seeing his size and obvious demeanour she turned to follow and protect her fleeing charges.

Elmer locked onto a medium sized female and quickly closed on her. Still quite young and inexperienced she ran in a blind panic, snatching a look behind to try and glimpse her pursuer she stumbled heavily over a large protruding tree root. Elmer was on her before she could get back up. The female boar squealed as he grabbed her by the back of the neck. Boar were deceptively strong and it took all of Elmer's weight and strength to hold her down. The female struggled violently and noisily for many minutes with Elmer having to constantly change his grip, had he picked a larger boar he may not have been successful but he knew his game, eventually she was subdued and fell quiet.

Elmer stood up, the now dead boar at his feet. The battle had been long and tiring. His chest heaved up and down as lungs worked extra hard to suck in more oxygen. He stood still, looking around for his father. Where was he? Elmer had expected him to join in the attack, to help if needed. He left the dead boar where it was and headed back towards his fathers last position. After only a few steps he stopped, something was approaching through the bushes ahead of him, it was large and moving at a steady pace straight towards him. Elmer planted his feet and stared hard into the rustling bushes. The dense greenery parted and Orin burst out, a lifeless piglet clamped firmly between his jaws. Elmer relaxed instantly, trotting forwards and pushing happily against his father's side.

In the confusion thrown up by Elmer's attack one of the fleeing piglets had run straight at his father and even he had managed to catch and kill it easily.

Elmer nudged his father again on the side of his head, then turned and trotted back to his own prize. His family would eat well today, two kills were a rare occurrence. Elmer and his father quickly settled down to eat their fill of meat from the larger carcass, this would make what was left light enough for Elmer to carry easily home. It was the first good meal Orin had eaten for many days; he savoured it.

As father and son approached the home site the large black pup could be seen standing alert at its entrance. On seeing the adults returning he squealed and rushed out, followed quickly by his sister. Elmer and Orin dropped the meat that they were carrying and accepted the welcome of the pups with swishing tails. The pups it seemed, had already accepted Orin, and this made Elmer feel even more happy about this day.

Freya emerged from the home site and laid down to watch the scene before her. Elmer trotted over and rubbed himself against her before toppling into her side, they both rolled around, growling and mouthing each other.

The pups often took solid food now, even though their bodies were still not good at digesting it yet. They ignored the dropped carcasses and both started licking and nudging feverishly at Orin's mouth. He responded by duly regurgitating a pile of steaming wild boar meat, and they both bolted it down.

Elmer jumped back up and trotted over to his pups. He received the same treatment as Orin, and like him also regurgitated another heap of warm meat on the ground. The female pup picked up a big piece and ran off to cache it, she didn't really need too as food was plentiful at the moment, but something inside her told her to do it; both she and her brother would bury some meat for later.

Freya trotted over now and after a quick nudge into Elmer' side walked over and laid claim to the larger boar carcass. She just managed to pick it up and retreated alone to eat her share.

After two more feeds on regurgitated offerings the full pups lay on their backs, all four feet pointing skywards, little, fat, temporarily swollen bellies on show. Freya had finished eating too, there was still some meat left on the boar carcass so she carried it quickly to a spot away from the den site, burying it for later.

With the meat cached she returned to the others, trotting over happily to Elmer and collapsing heavily into his side, they spent the next few hours in each others close company while the pups dozed contentedly away. Orin laid himself down some twenty metres away, not too close to annoy Freya but close enough to be part of things. He drifted off more content than he had been for many days.

Later, the whole family was dozing. Elmer was stirred from his nap as a movement registered in his half asleep eyes, they opened wide to see his father rising awkwardly from his laying position. It was obvious to him that his father was having trouble moving, his injuries were slowing him down. Elmer watched on as Orin shook himself wildly to try and loosen up his aching body before trotting off into the forest to be alone for a while, worried eyes watching him go. Elmer hoped that the company of his family with some good food and protection, might help turn things around for his father.

Evening came quickly. Orin was still off on his own and Elmer got purposely to his feet. Freya watched him out of the corner of her eye, recognizing instantly the subtle signs in his movements, she knew what was on her partners mind. Her own behaviour started to liven up in response and she sprung up in anticipation. Elmer quickly found the right spot. Sitting back on his powerful haunches he laid his massive head back onto his shoulders, his eyes closed gently and a look of pure enjoyment spread across his face as a long and beautiful howl rolled out across their land.

The still half asleep pups sprung eagerly to their feet and became instantly excited, they rushed around barging into each other, eyes on stalks as they looked for their next move. Elmer let out two more long howls, stopped and listened. Less than a minute later an equally beautiful howl returned from the forest around them. Orin was answering his son.

Freya was past excited now, she rushed around rubbing herself against the side of Elmer and nudging the pups, almost knocking them over. She finally settled into a sitting position beside her partner, pointed her head skywards and joined in.

All three adults were now in full flow, the harmonious howls exciting the pups so much that they were unable to stop themselves from joining in. Elmer was filled with joy, not just with the great feeling of howling with his family and father, but also with watching his pups trying to howl too; their disjointed howls and whines making him feel even better. The beautiful chorus carried on for several minutes, only coming to a halt when Orin stopped answering.

Elmer had started the howling to communicate with and check on his father, but he also did it because it made him feel good. He knew too that others would be listening, but this didn't worry him, for it told them that this was their land.

Orin returned later to the den site and laid down his normal distance away. Elmer got up and went over to him, the two pups following closely behind. He lay down gently beside his father and the pups not so gently, piled in. It was time for Orin to have his first proper interactions with Buster and Meg.

Buster the male pup, laid on top of Orin and Meg, the female pup, on top of Elmer. Freya trotted over and fell into the side of Elmer, knocking a disgruntled Meg to the ground. Orin shuffled himself around slightly to make Buster slide down his side and lay beside him; he was a bit on the heavy side for one so old and tired. Orin drifted contentedly off, loving the feeling of belonging again, to be accepted by Elmer's family. For now, all was well.

CHAPTER 8

NEAR MISS

Two more weeks had passed. The pups were now 8 weeks old and they ventured much further from the home site to explore and play. Elmer and Freya were often off hunting together now and Orin would stay behind to look after the pups.

Freya was unable to work out why she had come to trust Orin so quickly, maybe it was because he was so much like Elmer, she just seemed to know he would defend their pups with his life, even though they were not his. She did have some worries though. Orin was a large wolf in frame but not so strong in other ways, his condition, despite the good hunting of late, seemed not to be improving and she feared his physical strength in a time of need might be wanting. Freya reassured herself by instinctively knowing he would not flee and would fight to the end if needed. She and her pups could ask no more of him.

Today, Freya had set of behind Elmer to hunt and mark their territory. They had covered a couple of miles but she was hanging back, other things were on her mind. Freya came to a halt and shuffled around, facing back the way they had come. Elmer knew she had stopped and turned around to see why. She looked over her shoulder back at him and he knew straight away what was in her thoughts. He let out a gentle "woof," and she trotted off back towards her pups. Elmer turned back on to the animal track he had been following, it didn't bother him that he would hunt alone today, he often did, and so off he went.

Elmer stopped, raising his huge wet nose high into the air as a strong scent filled his nostrils. He purposefully moved his head around, sniffing in hard to try and pinpoint the source of it, ears swivelling around to search out sounds, while his eyes looked for movement in the depths of the surrounding woodland. Standing still and quiet he took it all in. Just seconds later he was off again.

His pace quickened slightly as he turned and trotted along a less well used track, sure in the knowledge that it would take him where he wanted to go. He travelled at an even brisker pace now, his objective becoming closer, tail wagging slowly from side to side at the increasing prospect of a hunt. Elmer knew he was almost there and slowed down to a walk, still scanning the woodland before him, trying to pin point his quarry. If Elmer could find him and remain undetected then surprise might remain on his side. There he was. A big old Red deer stag.

The stag may have been old, but he still looked in good condition. At well over twice Elmer's weight, with 18 points to his new velvet covered antlers, he was still a force to be reckoned with. The stag did not know the wolf was there yet and Elmer used this time to watch him closely, looking for any obvious tell tale signs that he may be weak in some way.

Elmer was not sure, the large size of the stag and his impressive weaponry was worrying him just a little. He decided to let the stag know he was there and see what happened, perhaps a tell might show itself when he was put under some pressure.

A stalking Elmer moved closer, but he did not move so quietly now. Only thirty yards away the stag sensed him and reacted, his huge well antlered head powering around quickly to face him. The deer's body swiftly followed his head and both were now eye to eye across the forest floor.

Elmer watched him with his predators eyes, running his gaze along the outline of deer's body looking for anything out of place, like a swelling or deformity, he watched closely every movement of the deer, looking for any awkwardness or signs that belied a deeper problem. The focused stag watched the wolf back with eyes that were experienced and seemingly unafraid. There was no sign of the old deer fleeing and both stood their ground. Elmer twitched his head slowly from side to side, could he hear some faint labouring in his opponents breathing, perhaps a slight sign maybe of some sort of weakness. If he could get the stag to run then maybe it would tell; but this foe had no intention of running.

The staunch old stag was a veteran of many situations like this. He knew that running from this big wolf would probably not be in his favour, and anyway, he had already made up his mind to stand his ground; hopefully his action would prompt the wolf to move on to find easier prey. The elderly male had not seen or sensed any other wolves yet and was somewhat bolstered up by the fact that this wolf, though big, was alone.

Elmer closed slightly and quickly on the deer to gauge his reactions, but the stag stood firm, lowering his head to the ground to emphasise his impressive weaponry and show his willingness to use them. Elmer had taken deer this size before on his own but he had known for sure that they were truly weak in some way. He had sensed something about this stag but seemed to know instinctively he would have to get him running hard to get some advantage. Elmer was now only 20 yards away and the stag still stood firm. He started to circle his foe and the deer turned tightly with him, keeping his impressive antlers pointing straight at the wolf.

The two circled together, predator and prey in a dance that had been carried out over millennia by their ancestors. The stag remained steadfast. Elmer was on the verge of giving up and moving on.

The old warrior, a winner of many such confrontations before, was getting frustrated by the continuous circling, his patience was wearing thin. With the wolf seemingly showing no signs of moving on he decided to take the initiative, and attack.

Elmer was taken completely by surprise as the old stag suddenly charged at him. Loose leaves and twigs that carpeted the forest floor now gave little grip as he scrambled to get traction and avoid the fast approaching antlers. He had made a big mistake and was now going to pay for it.

The stag covered the ground with surprising and ever increasing speed, lowering his head to the ground as he closed. He had caught the wolf out and would drive home his advantage. Years of rutting with other dominant stags and fighting off others like Elmer had made the old deer a hugely powerful animal in the short run. Elmer had precious little time to prepare himself.

The stag thrashed his antlers from side to side as he powered in, Elmer trying to stay between the two arms of pointed horn as he retreated. The deer pushed on hard, and Elmer found himself being trapped within the stag's antlers, in a prison of bone, being thrust backwards through the undergrowth with a power that surprised him.

Luckily for Elmer the elderly stag's antlers were exceptionally large, the gap between the stems on each side of his head was wide, and even a wolf of his size, with some frantic movements, was able to stay between them. The stags age and prowess, represented by his exceptional, well spread antlers, might just prove to be Elmer's salvation.

Leaves, twigs, mud and other forest detritus flew high into the air as Elmer tried in vain to get some purchase, to push back, but none came. The stag summoned up all of his strength to keep up his attack, hoping to drive the wolf into something solid like a tree stump or large root, so he could do some serious damage.

Elmer was now getting worried about the outcome. Thoughts of his young family, his father, and how they would cope without him flashed through his mind, and some extra strength from deep inside him, seemed to appear. He managed to lock onto the base of the bony antlers close to the stags head and started growling loudly in a bid to worry the deer, and also to help him try and summon even more power himself.

The ground seemed to become firmer, giving Elmer some grip, he pushed back with all his mite and felt it having some effect. For a moment the stag felt like he might be getting weaker, but only slightly, the situation was still grave. The deer momentarily lifted his head, raising Elmer easily into the air and dumping him down again hard on the ground, hoping to dislodge him and drive home an antler point. The stag could have backed away now and easily made his escape, but the blind rage of battle, and a hope of victory, had taken him over.

The usual forest sounds were being drowned out with the sounds of the life and death struggle, and all its creatures stopped to listen. Elmer's growling grew even deeper and fiercer as he fought for his life, one wrong move would cost him dearly. The deep snorting and grunting of the enraged old stag was equally loud as he searched within himself also for something to help sustain him. Billowy, white clouds of hot air escaped from both battling animals and hung eerily in the crisp clear air as they fought on. Only a minute had passed but it seemed like ages. Elmer called upon all that he had.

The stag suddenly stopped pushing. Elmer's mind for an instant wondered why, for he was surely losing this fight. Close enough to smell the stag's breath, Elmer could clearly see the look in his foes eyes turn from one of controlled, focused rage, to that of wide open surprise. The stag released Elmer from his prison, pulling back quickly and swinging his head round to see what it was that had caused the pain to his rear, removing him from a battle that he was winning.

A much smaller, snarling and bristling wolf, with intense eyes, looked back at him. Freya easily evaded the fast, stabbing antlers lunging towards her and retreated, leading the stag away from her partner. The stag now had two wolves before him, one strong and one fast, the odds were not so favourable now and there might well be more; did he want to stay and find out. Hot air shot forcefully from his flared nostrils as he snorted in defiance, considering his next move. The old warrior spun around quickly. Standing tall he quickly looked into the eyes of both wolves then trotted stiffly and strongly away, hoping his final show of strength would encourage this foe not to pursue him.

Freya was not impressed and looked to her partner, but Elmer was staying where he was. This would be one that got away. Freya could see Elmer was not interested in giving chase and padded over to be near him. Secretly, she was happy with his decision, something told her things might not turn out well if they followed this beast.

Elmer had learnt a lesson today, one that he would not forget quickly, luckily he had only received minor injuries that would heal quickly. He now knew even he was not invincible.

Earlier that day, Freya had returned to the home site after leaving her partner to hunt alone. Orin was in close attendance so she had a quick play with the pups then decided to retrace Elmer's tracks, finding him locked in battle. Her swift action had probably saved him from serious injury or worse and Elmer was well aware of it. He would have done the same for her though.

Together they now headed for the meadows on the edge of the woods, they held many rabbits and hares and they had become experts at catching them. Today, these much easier prey would be Elmer's choice.

It was late afternoon when Elmer and Freya returned to the home site, a hare and two rabbits in their jaws. Both had already eaten themselves while in the fields and the meal they now brought home, though not large, was eagerly awaited by the pups and Orin. The pups rushed out and fussed over their parents, before both grabbing the larger hare from their mum and trying unsuccessfully to pull it in half, they were not yet quite strong enough to do so, and after some further growling and posturing both settled down to share it. The pups would be having meals of fresh meat more often now. Elmer laid the two rabbits down near Orin and he gladly took them, with both rabbits hanging from his jaws he moved away a little to eat.

After eating both pups began to wind each other up, fuelled by the excitement from having just fed, it quickly led to a spell of vigorous play. The boisterous games only lasted for a few minutes before thoughts of a satiated snooze beckoned. Unaware of the grave fight their father had been through that day the pups assumed their usual positions; on their back all four feet pointing skywards, with Elmer, Freya and Orin close by.

Orin had noticed the injuries that his son now carried, but seeing he was unconcerned, drifted off too.

CHAPTER 9

ORIN

Another week had passed and to Elmer it seemed that as his pups put on weight and grew bigger, his father lost it and became smaller. Orin struggled sometimes to get to his feet, he was better once up and moving, but Elmer could see easily the pain and tiredness growing within him. Orin willingly and happily stood guard over the pups when Elmer and Freya were away hunting or patrolling their homeland and Elmer was happy that Orin was there, but his father's condition was worrying him greatly.

The injuries that Orin had received in the fight for his family and his home would have killed many a wolf. He had seemingly recovered from those physical injuries but now carried on a daily battle with an illness inside of him. Orin could feel himself losing that battle some days but was buoyed up by being with his son, and the playful and loving interaction with the pups. Even the pups though, had sensed the growing weakness within him, they played less heavily with their minder, especially Buster.

The infection in Orin's blood had taken hold and it would not let go.

Elmer and Freya returned to the home site carrying no food in their jaws. The pups rushed out, nudging and licking them around the muzzle, but they had nothing within them to give either, and the pups quickly got the message. Buster turned and trotted over to his babysitter, eagerly flopping onto his back beside him, then wriggling around so he was in a position to push himself away using Orin's body to thrust against. Orin responded by mouthing the pups back legs and pinning him gently with one of his huge front paws. Buster managed to wriggle free and started jumping madly around his playmate, in a bid to entice him to chase, but Orin stayed laying down. Buster headed off excitedly towards his sister.

Elmer padded over to his father, pushing his large head into his side, before lying down gently beside him. Orin revelled in these times of closeness with his son and they both pushed against each other; Elmer using little of his great strength. Freya watched them interact and could see plainly the compassion and respect that Elmer showed towards his father, and it somehow affected her, she had never seen such, so openly, before.

Father and son spent the next hour in each others close company until Orin decided to get slowly to his feet. He walked over to the now dozing pups and placed his huge head between them. Both licked and nudged him as he ran his nose over their little bodies. Orin gave them a few little nudges of his own back, sniffing in hard at the same time to savour their scents. He lifted his head up from them and looked over to Freya with a knowing gaze. Freya looked back at him with some compassion and admiration in her eyes, and he felt good for an instant; Freya seemed to know he was trying to say something. Orin then trotted over to Elmer for one last lingering rub against the side of his favourite son. Tail still wagging gently he turned and disappeared into the surrounding forest.

That night Elmer trotted a short distance from the home site and howled like never before, even more intense and mournful than after the loss of their little female. No answer came to his howls but he carried on his hopeful cries throughout the early evening. Freya wanted to join in but did not. The pups lay quietly and listened intently.

For the next few days the change in Elmer's behaviour was obvious to all his family. He still went off to cover and mark their home but often his head was low and his mood subdued. Freya too felt a sense of something at Orin's leaving but stayed alert; they still had their pups to look after. The pups knew too that something had happened to Orin, they often searched the forest around their home for their caring babysitter, but he was never to be found.

Elmer carried on his lone evening howling, on and off, for the next three days. On the fourth day he woke early. The family had slept near the entrance to the temporary den but not in it. He cast his eyes over his resting family and for a second looked for Orin, but he was not there. Elmer went off on his own, Freya watching him leave. She sensed he wanted to travel alone again.

Like the previous three days Elmer would travel to the very edges of their homeland. By the end of this day he would have travelled to the limits of their land in all directions and his search would be over.

A grieving Elmer had not done any hunting over the last few days so Freya ushered the pups into the relative safety of the temporary den. She gave the pups the look that said 'stay here' and set off to hunt. Now nearly 10 weeks old the pups were highly mobile and both, especially Buster, found it hard to stay put and not follow the adults whenever they went away. Another couple of weeks and they would be able too and actively encouraged to follow along, but for now Freya thought they were not ready.

Buster rose from his position next to his sister and trotted to the edge of the clump of trees that was their temporary home. He stood there looking out. The urge to follow his mother was great but so too was his fear of the telling off he might get. His sister lay back in the centre of the clump, knowing only too well what was on her brother's mind; she would let him get on with it. The desire was too much for him, and nose to the ground he trotted off in pursuit of his mum.

It was a warm sunny morning as Buster moved easily from shade to sunlight between the trees, his young but already considerable nose keeping him on track. The bold little pup trotted happily along, tail swishing slowly from side to side.

Buster stopped abruptly, his eyes screwing up just a little, allowing him to focus better on the big black spider that was moving slowly across the ground a few yards before him. Seeing a chance for some fun he sprang forwards, closing quickly on the big insect. The spider had already sensed the air shifts and vibrations caused by the rushing pup and knew it was something large and possibly dangerous, he froze on the spot.

Momentarily captivated, he dropped his nose to the ground and pushed it like a plough through the leaf litter towards the large insect. The spider, now knowing that staying still was not going to work, made a dash for it, and Busters front paws came crashing down around him. The spider focused all his bodily energy down into his legs, jumping with one large bound out of the young wolf's trap and into the nearby vegetation, quickly melting away. Buster was perplexed for a second, then started poking around in the grass with his nose, sniffing heavily, looking for his unwilling playmate, but he was gone. The little wolf set off again.

The audacious pup had already travelled about a mile from the home site, investigating anything that seemed worthy as he went. This was the furthest he had ever gone on his own and though he was being driven by the familiar and safe smell of his mother, something suddenly made him wary.

His swishing tail now became still as a feeling of something bad washed over him. His first instinct was to run back to the den, but he didn't. He stood still, calling on his new and inexperienced senses, trying to work out what it was that made him feel so. The little wolf pup knew he was being watched, and had a good idea where from.

He stared hard at some bushes not far ahead, trying to pick something out, but whatever it was did not want to be seen yet. Buster let out a 'woof,' as loud as his little lungs allowed, trying to make it sound like 'I know you are there,' but hidden inside it was also a hint of fear, and the unseen hunter recognized this.

The heavily leafed branches parted and a large dog fox stepped slowly onto the path. Just like a wolf, the orangey red canine was an opportunist hunter, this large experienced male would be able to take him easily. The fox moved strongly but cautiously forwards, if this wolf pups parents were about it would be him that would lose his life today. He too had young and a mate to feed, and this drove him on.

Buster could not win this battle. If he ran he would most certainly be caught and killed. If he did manage to make it to the den he would lead him to his sister, and with no adults at the den to protect them they might both be killed. He decided to fight for his life right here.

The experienced hunter was a little bemused that this youngster had not run, but stood his ground before him, and for an instance a flash of respect ran through his mind. The wolf pup was under two thirds his size with undeveloped jaws and teeth and little experience but he sensed it would not be as easy as he first thought; it would still though be no real contest and he moved in.

The wolf pup peeled back his lips and snarled as best he could, sinking back slightly on his haunches to receive the impact of the fast approaching hunter. The big male fox quickly covered half the ground towards the pup, Buster remaining still and unfaltering, preparing himself for the fight of his short life.

Something moving low and fast came in from Buster's right hand side, so fast that neither the fox nor the pup had time to properly register it. The gingery red attacker lifted up and flew sideways through the air with the force of the impact in his side. Leaf litter, twigs and dust flew high into the air as the fox landed heavily on the ground. Cripplingly winded and temporarily disorientated he didn't even have time to lift his head to see his attacker. Freya grabbed him by the back of his neck.

The fox knew instantly that it was all over for him. He struggled violently, thrashing his legs and letting out several long yelps, but it was over quickly. Freya laid down holding the fox in a death grip for several seconds, as if to make sure, but she knew he was already dead. She stood and ragged the dead fox in her jaws before dropping him to the ground. He would lie where he fell, food for the ravens and crows, and one less to scavenge from their kills she thought.

A relieved Buster had watched the foxes last moments, he was impressed with his mothers swift actions and the ease of her kill; she though was not so happy with him. Freya communicated her feelings towards him with one of her looks as he went to approach. Buster stopped and turned back, lowering his body slightly, tucking his tail firmly between his legs, and slinking off back towards the den. Now and then he risked casting a sheepish little look behind for his mum, hoping to be met with a more inviting look, but he never got one.

When Buster got back to the den his sister was up and waiting for him. She could tell something had happened but not that her brother had nearly lost his life that morning. With a wagging tail and some soft whines she comforted him, and he accepted it gratefully.

Freya didn't appear back at the home site until later, but went straight in to spend some time with the pups. As she rolled around with her pups Freya was hoping that her bold son had learnt a lesson today.

Elmer was still searching. He was just about to turn and make his way back to his family when a familiar smell drew his immediate attention. He followed the scent with his nose, already knowing what it was. Small whimpers seemed to come from him uncontrollably as he closed, his tail went down between his legs and his speed slowed until he was only just moving.

A fallen oak tree, one he regularly marked on, came into view, and his eyes focused in on the body that lay tightly under it's exposed roots. Elmer pushed his nose into his fathers side and there was no response. He pushed harder, and started to whimper loudly.

Elmer laid close beside his fathers body for over an hour, sometimes nudging him and often crying. He didn't want to leave him but knew he should be getting back to his own family. Elmer got up slowly and walked just a few metres away. The light was starting to fade and Elmer said his own last farewell. One long mournful and uninterrupted howl filled the forest, he carried on until only his own bodies lack of air caused him to stop.

Freya and the pups heard his howl. Freya knew straight away what it meant and found herself becoming inwardly emotional, letting a small whimper come out. The pups looked at her and could see the change in her, both came over to lick and nudge her.

Before he departed Elmer did his best to cover his fathers body, nosing leaves and twigs towards him and flicking them over him, then gently patting them down with his chin.

It was dark when Elmer returned to the normal greetings of his exuberant pups, it immediately made him feel just a little bit better. Tonight he would not howl but just spend it with his family. He now knew for sure that his father would never be coming back. After what had happened today Freya found herself thinking about Orin, had he been here Buster would not have strayed, and strangely, she felt some feelings about the misgivings she had thought of him.

Later that night a small vixen moved quietly around the forest eventually finding the body of her crushed partner. She stood beside him for a minute, quiet and subdued, saying good bye, then headed off back to her own little family. Life had just got much harder for her, but she was a born survivor.

CHAPTER 10

THE GOOD LIFE

The last month had been hard on Elmer and his family, one of their pups had died, and after a short but memorable reunion with Elmer's father, they had lost him too. Elmer had also come close to losing his own life, and may well have if not for his partners swift actions. He would learn from his mistakes of late. With a growing family to protect and provide for Elmer found himself thinking about his father, how long and good his life had been, and how he would wish to be just like him.

The pups were now highly mobile, and not far off from joining Elmer and Freya on their hunting trips. Today would not be one for hunting though. They would spend it around the home site area in the company of each other. Elmer loved days like this, even more so since the recent events in his life. He had to ensure the well being of his family and secure their homeland, things he approached always with great enthusiasm, boundless courage and devotion, but he truly loved spending time with his family, playing with the pups and being close to Freya. Soon they would have to start teaching the pups about the more serious ways of life for a wolf, but for today, play was top of the list.

Elmer sank down on his front paws in a deep play bow, his rear end high in the air and tail swishing slowly from side to side; an invitation impossible to refuse. Buster and Meg, wide eyes fixed with intent, took up low stalking stances, slowly approaching their father. He could see the hunter developing in their bright blue eyes and knew they would both be rushing him any second, his tail began swishing even harder as he waited for them to make their move.

Freya watched from a short distance away, loving the way her partner, this big powerful wolf, played with their little pups. All wolves loved to play with their own pups but she could see plainly the huge enthusiasm and affection within him.

Both pups rushed in. Buster jumped as high as his little legs would propel him and he landed awkwardly on his fathers head. Meg rushed to the rear, clamping down on her fathers long wispy tail and pulling for all she was worth. With Buster hanging on to one of his ears Elmer turned in a tight circle and playfully clouted Meg with one of his huge paws, sending her rolling away. He then lowered his head quickly, depositing Buster at his feet, and pinning him to the ground with his other paw.

Buster wriggled, squirmed and produced a few squeals as he fought to escape his fathers grip, for a short while he had an idea what it felt like for his sister when he pinned her to the ground. Elmer let him free and he raced off, tearing around the home site with reckless abandon, mouthing any object that came within reach. Freya did not escape from Busters moment of madness as he piled heavily into his mothers side. She grabbed him between her front paws and managed to hold onto him for a second, before he broke free and dashed of again.

Meg had clamped back onto her father's tail, holding on and growling loudly while he walked effortlessly around, dragging her behind him. Meg planted all four paws firmly in the ground, standing as tall and as strong as she could in a bid to slow her father, but to no avail. Elmer started moving faster and became joyous at the sight of the growling little pup flying around on the end of his tail. Buster could see his sister losing the battle to hold on and rushed over to help, growling deeply he grabbed hold of his fathers tail too.

Elmer stood still, pulling them both around by his tail might well become hard work, he rolled onto his back and just enjoyed watching them trying to move him. Buster already had a fair tug on him but he had no chance of moving his huge father. Elmer loved it.

Buster let go now, and taking advantage of his father being on his back grabbed one of his back legs and chewed on it, he then moved up to one of his front legs and bit on that. Meg followed Buster's lead, moving up to have a little chew on her fathers other front leg. Elmer was in heaven as all three of them growled playfully and rolled about. Now and then he would make a point of pinning one of them to the ground for a second or two and have a chew on their legs; just to remind them who was really the boss. The good feelings were welling up within Freya as she watched the play

66

between her partner and their pups, eventually the urge became too great and she padded over to join in.

Buster saw his mother coming and let go of Elmer's leg. He rushed around the back of Freya and started tugging on her tail. Freya swung around and Buster let go just before she had a chance to grab him, speeding off with his mum in close pursuit. As he ran Buster looked gleefully behind himself, pulling his tail in as tight as he could to his little body so as not to give her something to grab hold of. Not to be outdone she accelerated hard and swiped one back leg from under him. He done a few sloppy rolls, legs flying everywhere, then jumped back up and shot off again.

This time Buster headed into the bushes. He was still small enough to run under them and she would have to wait for him to come back out in the open. Buster glared at his mum as he sped around under the bushes, he could see she couldn't catch him in here and so ran even faster, his way of saying, 'can't catch me.' All was going well for him when 'Bang!' He ran into a fair sized immovable trunk and it stopped him dead in his tracks. The feel good hormones pulsing through his body allowed him to ignore the temporary pain and he exploded back up and off again, this time out into the open and a waiting Freya. She quickly caught up, rolling him, then pinning the wriggling pup to the ground, she held him there just long enough to say, 'I could catch you any time really.'

The intense play carried on for over an hour before the pups collapsed exhausted into a heap beside their parents. Elmer thought he had noticed a difference in the way Freya was playing with the pups, it seemed more intense and he thought he saw real enjoyment in her, more than he had noticed before. In some situations of late she seemed more mellow and softer. He would not want to change her but found himself admiring this new side of her greatly.

Freya herself had also been thinking about her behaviour of late and wondered if recent events, especially where Orin was concerned, were having some effect on her. Whatever was taking place she had revelled in watching and playing with her pups and it now seemed somehow even more enjoyable to her.

Play was good for all the family and it also helped greatly with the pup's social development, fitness and strength. Many of the moves they used in play might well be employed later in more serious times. Elmer loved what he was seeing, it was a real tonic to him, he would never tire of days like today. Their pups were growing quickly and he would ensure that there would be many days like today while they were young. The family spent the rest of the day playing and resting.

Life felt good again.

CHAPTER 11

THE FIRST HUNT

It was a bright and sunny morning with a strong cooling breeze. The sun was hanging low in the sky, casting long dark shadows far and finger like across the forest floor, as if trying to search something out. Today was the day. The pups would join their parents on their first hunting trip.

Both Elmer and Freya were becoming excited by the prospect ahead and they busily moved around, nudging their eager pups and vocalising with high pitched whines, squeals and growls. The pups, especially Buster, were whipping themselves up into a little frenzy, they seemed to know what was about to take place, and couldn't wait to get moving.

The excitable behaviour became noisier and more intense until Elmer was ready to go. He stood still and quiet for a second then shook his whole body violently to release the pent up excitement within him. With a more purposeful look now emanating from him, he trotted slowly off, tail swinging slightly from side to side.

Buster copied his father, shaking his little body hard and taking on a similar serious look, then after standing as tall as his frame would allow, trotted off after him, uncontrollable little tail circling madly behind. Meg looked to her mother for some reassurance. Freya gave her young daughter a soft reassuring 'woof ' back and an instantly happier Meg trotted off to catch up with her brother. Freya brought up the rear. She would stay here for a little while until the pups got used to following, then move up behind Elmer. Freya looked up the file of her little family as they trailed off before her and the good feelings flooded in, her tail swished forcefully from side to side not just at this sight ahead of her, but also at the anticipation of an imminent hunt; she truly loved to hunt.

The family had covered a couple of miles and Freya thought the pups were doing well keeping up, she put on a short spurt and passed them to take her place behind Elmer. Meg didn't want to be at the back on her own so she accelerated past Buster and stayed a few yards behind her mum. Buster was quite happy being at the back, occasionally stopping to investigate something, briefly smelling or nudging it before running to catch up. Freya often looked back over her shoulder to make sure the pups were still following while Elmer concentrated on what was ahead; even from that distance Buster could feel her stare and it would make him tow the line, for a little while.

Elmer stopped and Freya followed suit. The pups almost caught right up with the adults before they realised they had halted. Just like their parents, both pups now stood dead still and tried using their own senses to work out what it was that had brought them all to a standstill. Elmer moved forwards much slower than before, more deliberate, stopping frequently to scent the air and listen. The pups watched his and Freya's every move. The family left the track they were on for a smaller one and headed down it. Elmer's speed increased a little and the pups could sense the rush to get to whatever was ahead; they could smell things now too.

The faster and more active trotting carried on for a few minutes until they reached a very large clearing. Elmer stopped in the tree line on the edge of the glade and Freya came up silently beside him. The pups copied their parents and quietly they moved up behind them. Freya gave them one of her looks and they both sat quietly, their little tails slowly swishing away in anticipation of what might come. The adults moved slowly forwards to the almost edge of the tree line.

In the centre of the clearing stood a small herd of fallow deer, a mix of last years young with their mothers and some older females. Elmer had done his job well, the wolf family had approached the group from the downwind side and had remained undetected. Both scanned the area and the prey before them for several seconds then without any noise Freya prepared to move off. After giving the pups another one of her 'stay there' looks she went back into the trees to slowly make her way through the forest, around to the opposite side of the clearing. It would take her some time.

As Freya moved she kept herself ready to run, the deer could possibly smell her at any time and their reaction to this would be her trigger to rush in. Hopefully, if they were lucky, one of the deer would try to make good its escape in the direction of her partner.

Elmer moved out a short distance into the clearing to some longer grass, he moved slowly and deliberately towards his chosen spot and after reaching it unseen, lay down and waited. The pups, even though they had been given the look, moved slightly forward to try and get a better view; they were both highly driven to watch the well rehearsed behaviour taking place before them.

Buster was finding it harder and harder not to move even closer. His little tail moved quicker and quicker from side to side behind him. It was all too much. He stood up and padded over to a fallen tree on the edge of the clearing. Keeping his back legs on the ground he jumped his front legs up onto the old trunk. His head was higher up now and he could get a better view. Meg hesitantly followed him over and joined him. The two of them now stood upright, side by side, looking like two little bear cubs trying to see more, both their tails swishing around freely as they eagerly watched their parents in action.

Freya had almost circled around to the far side of the deer when they smelt her. One of the deer gave out a warning, lifting a front leg to chest height, then stamping it's cloven hoof down hard into the ground, she followed this up quickly with a short, sharp bark. All the deer's heads swivelled around to look in Freya's direction. Freya stayed statue like as she watched them scanning the area where she hid, their ears erect, bodies tight and tall; they were deciding how to react, for sure they would run.

Freya wanted to rush them before the deer decided to take off themselves, hopefully allowing her to influence their choice of escape route, ideally towards her hidden partner. She quickly scanned the clearing around the deer. The ground to the left was much denser with some uneven ground, not good for these smaller deer, so she assumed they would decide to go to the right. If she could make her initial charge to the right side she might force them to go to the left, they would not want to go into the rougher area and so might then decide to flee straight back behind them, staying on the flatter, less tangled ground, and into Elmer.

She made up her mind in seconds and inched forwards to the very edge of the trees. Leaning slightly back on her coiled up back legs she chose her moment and exploded forwards. Freya didn't run straight at

71

the deer but well to their right, her great speed saw her cover many metres before the deer assessed the situation and reacted.

The strategy was working. As a herd animal the deer reacted as one and followed the lead doe. The dominant does instincts followed the reckoning of Freya. The deer ran away from the wolf, but not wanting to run into the rough ground and maybe get tripped the dominant doe turned again and headed straight back down the middle of the clearing, keeping the rough round on one side and the wolf on the other.

Elmer decided he would stay hidden until the last moment and take out the deer that came closest to him. Freya was still moving down the right hand side to herd them towards him and it was working well. The deer were moving fast, even Elmer would feel the impact from one of the larger of these medium sized deer, they were almost as heavy as him. He prepared himself.

The pups watched intently the scene before them, they had never seen their mother move so fast and both were in awe of her speed. They had watched their father lay down and knew exactly where he was. The lead deer was heading straight towards him.

Elmer would take the first deer. She was the largest and moving flat out, and even he now thought a head on collision might not go well for him. Elmer decided he would rise up just before she reached him, hopefully making her slow and turn quickly, giving him the edge. At the worst he should be able to slow her up greatly giving Freya time to join him.

The lead doe was only twenty feet from Elmer when he sprung up from his hiding place. She planted her front feet in an attempt to slow and give her time to turn and avoid him but her momentum was too great, quickly changing her mind she decided to jump straight over the big wolf before her.

Elmer had read things well and he exploded upwards hitting the doe hard under her back legs as she went over him. The force of the impact made Elmer wince, but the surging adrenaline rush that always accompanied such situations, allowed him to ignore it. The doe cart wheeled through the air and landed hard behind him, she too though was being driven by some powerful hormones, ones for flight; dazed and ignoring any pain she quickly tried to get back to her feet, but was not fast enough.

The other deer in the herd flew past without looking back as Elmer grappled with his flailing prize. He got a good grip of her neck just as Freya joined him. The doe was still strong but the extra weight of Freya allowed Elmer to pull her easily down, it was soon all over. Freya might have been able to catch another, smaller deer, but she wanted to make sure they kept this one.

Sure that the doe was now dead and would not pose any threat to the pups Freya let out a loud 'woof,' to call them in. The excited pups rushed out from the tree line, greeting their parents with high pitched squeals and whines. They rushed around pushing their heads into their parents, not just excited about what they had seen, but also happy that both their parents had come safely out of the encounter, and a large meal now lay before them. Elmer and Freya would let the pups eat first.

Buster calmed down first and approached the deer's body. He walked around it, little tail still swishing away sporadically behind him, stopping every few strides to smell and poke it with one of his paws. He paused occasionally to look back to his parents for some guidance, but Elmer and Freya didn't move; they wanted to see how the pups coped on their own for a bit.

Meg came over now, she wasn't quite as openly enthusiastic as her big brother to start with but soon found her courage rising in line with Busters growing interest. Both the pups knew this was food laying before them, but they had to get into it.

Buster tried first. Grabbing the rear end he tugged on it with all his mite. The carcass stretched a little but stayed exactly where it was, he just about marked the hide and that was it. Little growls filled the air as the pup became obviously frustrated at his failure. Buster carried on determinedly jerking away, but it wasn't long before his jaws and teeth were aching. He wasn't yet up to opening the thick hide on a deer's rump. Meg decided to have a go now, and not learning from her brothers failed attempt she also tried on the deer's rump, with the same results, an exhausted pup.

After watching the pups pulling frantically at the carcass for several minutes Freya came trotting over, she had seen enough, and quickly opened the carcass up for them. Both pups watched intently as mum made short work of it, going for the thinner skinned areas underneath; another lesson for them. Elmer stayed where he was for now, happily watching his pups feed to bursting point on their first proper kill. There was enough meat here for a couple of days.

The usual suspects had already started to arrive in the trees nearby but they would have to work hard to get a share from this kill. Freya would be extra vigilant with the pups around; a raven could do some damage with it's sizeable dagger like beak to an exuberant and inquisitive pup, and she hated them anyway.

The pups first experience of a hunt and kill had gone well, the tactics that Elmer and Freya used had worked well for this size of deer. If the deer had been a bigger species, like Red deer, they would have had to use different tactics as Elmer might have been seriously injured in the first contact. The way Freya herded the deer towards Elmer was good for the pups to watch, though luck, as in many hunts, often played a role.

Serious injury when hunting larger prey is always a risk for wolves and can easily become life threatening event, Elmer and Freya had to constantly assess every hunting opportunity that they came across and employ the right tactics; one's that only came with experience and learning. Most hunting for Elmer and Freya would take place in dense woodland, as this covered most of their territory, it required different tactics from hunting in wide open spaces. There were some occasions though when they might not have time to think about tactics or assess the situation properly, sometimes they could literally stumble upon hidden prey and have to decide quickly how to handle it, it was never a foregone conclusion, but with Elmer's strength and Freya's skilful speed, most prey would have to look out.

The first lesson could not have gone better.

CHAPTER 12

MORE LESSONS IN LIFE

The family had spent the last few days close to the now well eaten carcass, only some of the larger bones, pieces of tough skin and a bright red stain on the ground gave a trace of it.

Buster trotted over to the remains and picked up the largest bone around, he tried to balance it in his jaws but every time he went to move off the bone tipped up and one end stuck in the ground. It took several goes before the visibly disgruntled pup found a point of near balance, success instantly changing his outward appearance to one of excitement.

He trotted over to Meg and proceeded to push the large bone repeatedly into her face. It took five or six prods before his sister responded, grabbing the other end of the long leg bone in her jaws. This would be the start of a twenty minute tug of war, one which Buster could win easily, but he did just enough to keep Meg interested.

Meg knew she would not be able to beat Buster in any tug of war and after a few minutes she changed tactics. Her growling turned from one of excitement and play to one more of frustration and aggression. She was hoping her brother would see the hopelessness within her, that she was getting more aggressive because she couldn't win, and hopefully he would then give in because he felt a bit sorry for her.

Today though, Buster was having none of it, and he continued to drag her around on the end of his bone. The war of the bone soon became one of great importance and neither wanted to give up. Meg hung on stubbornly as Buster, though the strongest, became visibly weaker with the effort of dragging the bone and Meg around.

Minutes later and temporarily exhausted they both had to stop and regain some strength. The bone lay still on the ground, a heavily breathing wolf pup clamped securely to each end, low growls rumbling from both of them.

The intenseness of the situation was temporarily defused as the eyes of both pups simultaneously looked upwards and focused on the brightly coloured butterfly that had stopped for a moment to dance around in the air above them, the beautiful insect blissfully unaware of the little battle of wills taking place on the ground below it. Buster was now in a bit of a dilemma. Did he keep battling for his bone or relinquish it to his little sister and try and catch the butterfly. Meg could see the turmoil taking place inside her big brother's head and waited to make her move, willing him to chase the butterfly.

The red admiral butterfly fluttered down invitingly to within a few feet of Buster and he could resist no longer. He let go of the bone and sprung upwards as high as his tired little legs would propel him. The butterfly, seemingly forewarned of the impending danger, floated up effortlessly out of reach. Buster landed and puzzled for a second over his predicament, unable to work out how an insect that looked like it had no eyes was able to move just out of his grasp when he tried to catch it.

This was what Meg had been waiting for and she excitedly snatched up the bone, dragging it quickly under a nearby low bush, covering it with her body and growling loudly, announcing to all her possession of it.

Buster was now oblivious to the plight of the bone. Captivated by the dancing insect he followed it into the woods, launching himself skywards whenever he thought there might be a chance of catching it, and becoming increasingly frustrated when it always managed to stay just beyond his outstretched paws. Five minutes later and the young wolfs antagonist fluttered high into the trees and disappeared. Buster returned to the rest of the family and with a huge resigned sigh slumped himself down a few feet from Meg, who was happily gnawing away on his bone, with that look in her eyes.

Elmer and Freya had spent the last few hours lying side by side watching the antics of their young family, it amused them both. As they lay there Elmer cast his eyes over his mate, her coat, like his, had been shed now; they had always been in great condition and now they looked like it again. The smells and signs of Mother Nature were all around and Elmer took the time to watch and soak things up.

Summer was well into its season now, some of the spring flowers with their distinctive smells had long gone, but many of their underground bulbs lay dormant now, waiting to be found by foraging boar, bear and badgers. The young of many animals were born in the summer months and prey was usually plentiful. Elmer and Freya would soon be teaching their charges how to hunt more of them, but some lessons would still be learnt by the pups own trial and error.

Buster was getting bored. Leaving Meg to her bone he headed off on his own to the explore their woods, to see what was about. Travelling a path he already knew well the pups eyes busily scanned the ground before him, while his nose scented the air and his ears listened for anything of note. Just over three months old now he looked like a little wolf and travelled with much more presence and purpose than he had done, just weeks before. In this short time he had learnt many lessons about life and this land that surrounded him, but often the playful pup within him still took over, he couldn't help himself. Anything the intrepid pup thought worthy of investigation caused him to stop and take a closer look. He was still the boldest of pups. Buster trotted on.

Rounding a small bend in the path something ahead of him caused him to stop. Standing completely still his forehead wrinkled up in concentration and his eyes screwed up as he zoomed in on the unknown thing before him. To any that might be watching the big pup looked frozen, only his twitching nose moved as it searched for some scent, but none that he recognised could be found.

The creature before him did not move. Had it heard, seen or smelt him? Buster thought not. He moved in, taking slow deliberate steps, placing each paw down in its chosen place so as not to give himself away. The animal was long and thin and remained still in its sunny position. As he closed on the creature something within him was urging caution. He was just a few steps from it when the strange creature came to life. Buster could now make out the zigzag pattern running down the back of the brownish body and the deep black shape on the back of its head.

The snake turned slowly and slithered off with an easy, wave like motion, the way it was moving intrigued the inquisitive pup. The animal made it's way slowly from it's sunny exposed position to the shadowy and cooler undergrowth on the edge of the path. With half of it's body into the vegetation and half still on the path Buster moved in for an even closer look. Instinct and his experiences to date were telling him that the rear end of this unknown animal might pose less threat to him than the head end; an association that he had already had with most creatures as the head usually housed their weapons.

The serpent had almost made its way completely into the brush. Standing over the end of its fast disappearing tail the fascinated pup was unable to control his urges, one front paw shot out and pinned the last few inches to the ground. The snakes head coiled around on itself and struck out with lightning speed. Buster instinctively released it, at the same time bouncing back quickly away from it, his fast, youthful reactions, saving him from being bitten.

The response of the unknown creature had taken the wolf pup by surprise. The startled youngster regained his composure and then showed his worry by barking loudly at this thing that now moved towards him.

The female snake had been nonchalantly basking in the sun. Being a cold blooded animal she had to take in heat from the environment to warm her body up before she could set off on her daily travels. The warmth she had already absorbed today gave her greater speed. The snake had been enjoying her spot in the sun, but had given it up when disturbed, she would usually have disappeared into the brush if left alone, but not this day.

Buster could have simply gone on his way but the young male wolf within him now recognised some sort of challenge from this creature and he proceeded to bounce stiff legged around it, barking and growling loudly all the time.

Elmer responded instantly to the first bark he heard from his son, the sound of it telling him all he needed to know; his son was in trouble. Buster was about half a mile away, a distance Elmer could cover in well under a minute. He took off. Employing all his senses as he ran Elmer homed in on his son. Like most travelling wolves the youngster had used well worn paths where possible to allow for easier movement. His father now moved flat out along them.

Buster and his adversary were in the centre of the woodland path now, the snake stabbing out when it thought the pup close enough and the little wolf darting in and out, unaware of the danger he was in, this snake was unusually aggressive.

Leaves, twigs and mud from the forest floor flew high into the air as Elmer skidded onto the path that Buster was on, his speed increasing further still as he closed on his son. He could see Buster now, bouncing around on the path ahead of him, barking and growling at something on the ground. Temporarily reassured by his sons apparent lively condition Elmer pressed on. Buster could see his father approaching now, his barking and growling became even louder in anticipation of his mighty fathers help.

Even before he reached his son Elmer had a good idea about the type of foe that he was probably soon to be facing. Memories of watching a litter mate from his own birth pack being bitten by one of these creatures and becoming gravely ill came back to him, he knew only too well the possible danger that confronted him. As Elmer closed in a plan of attack went through his mind, would he slow, stop and then harass the snake into withdrawal, or would he pile in grabbing the snake and hopefully killing it. He decided quickly on a mix of both.

The snake had very limited long distance senses and being focused on the black wolf pup before him was completely unaware of the approaching adult wolf.

In his haste to protect his son Elmer came in too fast, he planted his huge paws firmly in a bid to slow himself, but the loose ground gave him little purchase and he slid towards the rear of the snake. Elmer had to think quickly. He snatched the snake up as he passed with a strong bite to its tail, and with a powerful flick of his head threw it up and over himself, into the undergrowth behind. The snake, taken almost completely by surprise, didn't have time to react.

Father and son stared together into the thick grass. The bewildered snake lay still for a minute, trying to work out what had just happened, getting its bearings, before slithering off quickly into the dense undergrowth. Buster made a move to pursue it but was shouldered to the ground by his father. The bold pup could see the intenseness in his fathers eyes as they drilled a message into him, 'Leave well alone.'

Buster got to his feet and shook the feelings of anxiousness out of him. The look on his face and his timid body language told Elmer that he now realised the seriousness of what had just happened. Elmer hoped, but was not assured, that his son had learnt another important lesson today. They turned together and headed back to the others. Buster trotted along just a little bit worriedly behind his father, but still had thoughts to stop and investigate things, something told him that now would not be a good time, better just to follow his father closely.

Freya was stood looking in the direction of Elmer and Buster when they returned. She had stayed to look after Meg and knew something of note had taken place when Buster rushed past Elmer and buried himself into her side. She spent a few minutes reassuring and playing with him. Meg jumped up, leaving her hard won bone, and trotted over to join in. She too, knew something serious had happened.

CHAPTER 13

HUNTING SCHOOL

Elmer trotted along confidently at the head of his family with Freya behind him, Buster in third place and Meg bringing up the rear. It was dusk and the light was fading slowly, but they could still see well. Elmer was taking them to the meadow lands that fringed their forest, these ancient fields, full of long grasses and wild flowers, covered the ground from the forest edge to the foot of the small mountains that lay to one side of their homeland.

Still a fair distance from his objective Elmer brought the file to a halt, Freya coming up beside him to see why. The pups stood together behind their parents wondering what was going on. As usual it was too much for Buster and he trotted slowly up and stood between them. He didn't get told off so Meg moved up and joined him. All four now stood side by side looking down the small forest path that stretched out ahead of them. The reason for their sudden stop then trotted into view.

A medium sized four legged animal, a bit smaller in height but bulkier than Meg, was making it's way casually up the path towards them. Elmer and Freya knew what it was but it was new to the pups. Buster was intrigued, it walked with a sort of barrelling side to side movement, and even at a distance some sort of confidence seemed to exude from it. The creature was seemingly oblivious to the small family of predators ahead of it.

The wind came from behind the approaching animal into the wolves faces and so it had no scent to warn it. The wolf pack stood completely still and silent, there was no movement or sound to give them away. It was a badger. Both Elmer and Freya knew that it's eyesight was not good and if they remained still it would not see them until almost upon them, it's other senses though were much better.

The old badger walked this path every evening, he had come across the sign of wolves before but this would be his first time he had experienced a close encounter. Like all of his kind he had his regular routes that he stuck too throughout his life and it would take something of great consequence to make him change it. Badgers underground homes, setts, were often used by their families over many generations, only abandoning them in extreme circumstances and so making them creatures of habit. When there were wolves about though, they had to be more careful.

The approaching badger was a big boar. He was a prolific eater of underground bulbs, tubas and worms, but would not pass by some carrion if he was lucky enough to find some, or steal it off a fox. He had few natural predators and was not regularly on the wolves list of prey. A lone wolf could kill a badger but it was never easy, they were deceptively strong, had powerful jaws and very sharp claws that they used to dig easily through sun baked earth. They could take a lot of damage before succumbing and they were capable of inflicting some too if a wolf was not careful, all in all they were a tenacious and sometimes aggressive little beast that did not give up easily when cornered.

No doubt when this one did eventually work out what stood before him he would take off back the way he came, but Elmer had already decided he would not take it on, they did not taste good anyway, and there was much easier prey around at the moment. For now he would let the pups watch this feisty character approach them and see what they made of it.

The badger was only about twenty yards away now and Elmer could see the inquisitiveness within both his pups. Had they been a few months older and more experienced he might have let them find out for themselves what these animals were like, but he ruled it out; it might not turn out well.

Both pups were looking at their parents and then back to the approaching black and white creature wondering what it was that they should be doing about it. They felt like rushing forward but restrained themselves as they could see this was not on their fathers mind. They pondered why.

Had the eyesight of the badger been as good as the wolves he would have seen them long ago but now only fifteen yards away he sensed something ahead of him. He froze on the spot with one front leg still halfway through it's travel. The little black and white barrel like creature stood there looking just like a wolf did as it scanned for some hidden prey ahead of it. He quickly sniffed the air and cocked his head from side to side to try and hear or smell something, but nothing came to him. Not being able to tell what it was he assumed it must be something that didn't want to be identified, perhaps a predator.

The old boar clumsily but quickly shuffled himself around and took off back the way he came, moving as fast as his short little legs would carry him. Buster and Meg's innate prey drive instinct took over and although Elmer didn't want it, they took of after him. Elmer and Freya followed on quickly after the pups, just in case they might need their help if they did manage to corner him.

The pups, though still young, were already faster than their quarry, and they were soon up behind him. The experienced boar though was a veteran of the trials of life and knowing that running was not going to work turned and backed into some heavy brush. Face on and only inches from his pursuers he could see they were only young wolf pups snapping away at him, but he could also make out that the other wolves behind were not. He turned again and bulldozed his way through the heavy brush behind him, it was thick and a little thorny but he didn't feel anything as he crashed through it.

Buster jumped forwards and poked his head into the temporary small tunnel that the fleeing badger had made, he could hear him smashing his way through the thick undergrowth and decided not to follow.

All the family had become a little excited by the short chase and after some whining and several long looks down the badgers hastily made escape route, they calmed down and moved off again. As Buster travelled he thought about the new animal he had just seen and was somewhat impressed by the way it had handled itself. For the next few minutes he carried this thought with him, then it drifted away having made some sort of impression on him.

It was almost dark when they reached the meadows. The family stood quietly on the edge of the tree line and scanned the ground around them for any sign of movement, the pups concentration looking just as focused as their parents. Buster and Meg watched their parents intently as they surveyed the scene before them, deciding on their next actions.

Both pups knew a hunt would soon be taking place and were becoming excited by the thought of it.

The meadow held many young rabbits and they were still sitting out in the last of the daylight, eating while hidden. Rabbits had excellent senses with almost all around vision and they were hard to sneak up on. Most of the rabbit warrens here could be found amongst the tree line or on the edge of the meadows, this meant that once a rabbit had detected a predator they would either have to try and get back to their nearest bolt hole or stay well hidden in the grass and hope to be passed by.

Elmer and Freya knew that when they did go out into the field many of the rabbits would make the dash back to their burrows, this was always the case, but they also knew that some of the younger, inexperienced one's, would lay still and hunker down, not even moving when the wolf was right on top of them. It would be these that they would target tonight.

Both wolves had both done this many times before and it was always productive at this time of year. Spring and into summer was the main breeding time for rabbits, they rarely lived longer than a year, producing four or five litters of kits, and started breeding from a very young age; they were a good, reliable source of food.

Elmer and Freya had both learnt the same way of hunting rabbits. They would walk slowly into and around the field as if not really interested. To some of the hiding rabbits it would look like they might just be passing through, most would flee but some would stay. Both wolves would continually scent the air while on the move trying to get a fix on a hidden rabbit. Once one of them was sure of the position of their hiding prey they would trot past very close to it and then suddenly dive into the undergrowth and grab it. Elmer had been taught to hunt rabbits like this by his own parents. Freya, over the past few months, had learnt it from Elmer. Now they would teach these tactics to their own offspring.

Freya gave Buster and Meg the usual look and Meg sat down straight away. Buster stayed standing, an expectant look on his face and his tail moving around even more than his sisters, he knew a lesson about hunting was coming.

As Elmer and Freya pushed out into the meadow a buck rabbit sat on top of a small hillock saw them straight away. The alert male was the

84

designated lookout for his warren today, keeping an eye out while his brethren ate with their heads down. The lone sentinel sat up tall then slammed one of his back paws down hard, several times, into the baked soil. The resulting noise and the vibrations that travelled through the ground gave a warning of imminent danger to any nearby members of his warren. The sentry then took off for the nearest bolt hole himself, as he fled the large white patch on his rump flashed away, serving as an extra visual warning to those that had not heard or felt his thumping.

In seconds the buck was down his hole, followed quickly by many of the other rabbits in his vicinity, some of them giving their own thump as a warning before they ran. An outward ripple of fleeing rabbits could be seen making its way across the meadow.

The wolf pair ignored this fast running prey and stuck to their well rehearsed tactics. Buster and Meg had been watching closely, and on seeing the rabbits flee before their parents both had jumped forward in a reflexive response to chase; they just managed to stay put. Freya's nose had picked up on something and she criss crossed the immediate area to get a better fix on it, moving downwind to be sure of it's position. Convinced now of where her prey was hiding she trotted towards it, but slightly to it's side.

The young rabbit hunkered down tightly as the wolf approached. Freya passed just three foot away from the well hidden kit and when almost past pounced sideways with one bound, landing almost on top of it. The young rabbit had no choice now but to try and escape, but Freya was quicker.

She grabbed it and a large mouthful of grass at the same time, the rabbit screamed loudly as she bit down and it was quickly dispatched. Freya carried it back to the pups and deposited it at their feet then returned to the hunting grounds. She heard another rabbit squeal to her side as Elmer was successful too.

The rabbits were small but everything would be consumed. Within a few hours the whole family had eaten some and the pups had learnt another valuable lesson. Next time they came here to hunt they would take the pups out with them for a closer look.

For at least the next year Elmer and Freya's lives would revolve around teaching and protecting these pups. New pups were the most important things to any wolf pack. They cherished them.

CHAPTER 14

IT'S NOT ALL PLAY

The early morning was bright and sunny. The suns rays already had a little warmth in them and the dawn chorus of the forest bird life was beginning to fade. Elmer had been laying awake for some time, soaking up the warmth and the good feelings. Today, he found himself unusually captivated by the beautiful sounds of the tiny feathered creatures around him.

Elmer laid on his front, huge head resting motionless on his outstretched front paws. Big golden eyes were the only things moving as his gaze wandered slowly from one member of his sleeping family to the other. His stare fell on Buster. The big pup's eyes opened wide and looked straight at him; not everyone else was asleep this early morning.

Father looked hard at son and for the first time Elmer registered properly the fact that his sons eyes were still blue. Meg's eyes had already turned from the wolf's blue birth colour to golden yellow, perhaps his son's eyes would always be blue, Elmer had seen it before in another adult wolf.

Buster stayed still, apart from his tail, which began to swish slowly from side to side at the eye contact with his father. Elmer knew if he carried on looking at his son he would come over. It was early but he loved any interaction with his pups; so he carried on staring at him. Buster rose slowly to his feet and after a little shake trotted over sheepishly to his father, it was as if didn't know quite how he might react. He need not have worried. Still laying, Elmer's tail started to swish powerfully from side to side behind him, small twigs and leaves that laid in it's arc swept easily aside.

Buster noticed his fathers inviting tail swipes, his eyes opened even wider with anticipation and he sped up, covering the small distance between them quickly, then toppling purposefully and heavily into his father's side. The early morning bliss was shattered by the sound of their playful growling and rough play.

The rumbustious noises of father and son woke Freya and Meg from their slumber, and without any attempt to loosen up Meg rushed over to join in. She didn't want to miss out on some play with her father.

Lately play within the family was embarked on with more tenacity than previously. Both pups were now strong enough for much rougher play, especially between themselves, and on occasion it would need the intervention of Freya to sort things out. This morning was to become one of those times.

Buster was not happy that his lone play with his father had been interrupted by his sister and the small wrestle that he was having with her about it quickly became more intense and noisy.

Freya could sense the change in the tone and intensity of her pup's growls and as Elmer looked like he would do nothing about it she trotted over. Normally, she would just let them get on with it, but something told her she should bring an end to it.

Standing tall and growling deeply she bared her teeth and forced her way between them. Both pups reacted the same, backing away slightly and lowering their bodies to the ground, tucking their tails between their legs. They looked up sheepishly towards Freya, their tongues darting in and out licking their own faces and the air around them in submissive and appeasing gestures. Freya needed to do no more, she would never really hurt them but sometimes they had to be told; when they got older though, reprimands would carry more weight. Elmer was always happy to let his partner deal with any unruliness of the pups but occasionally when he felt the need, usually it was about safety, he would have his say too.

Elmer had decided that they would leave their homesite for good this afternoon. Buster and Meg would be with them always now, and for the next eight months they would lead a more nomadic existence around their territory. Life would revolve around finding temporary sites as they travelled in areas that were near prey, water or shelter. The pups were growing fast and eating more now, even the largest of prey would only last a few days. Buster and Meg were still too young to add any real help to a hunt, they still had much to learn, but both parents thought their pups would be quick learners. Elmer and Freya both relished the challenge that their new family provided; it seemed to them that this was what they were here for.

Elmer made a point of playing even more with both his pups over the next few hours before they headed out. Freya joined in a few times but her mind was already elsewhere. She had an inkling that they would be leaving soon and her thoughts of the forthcoming search for prey were foremost. She loved her family, but Freya also loved to hunt.

Elmer rose quickly to his feet, the speed and purposefulness of it telling the pups that playtime was over. All the family became excited with the expectancy of moving off. The air filled with excited squeals, whines and short little howls, as they nudged and rubbed against each other, the fervour building until Elmer thought it was time to leave. He stood stock still for a few seconds before shaking his whole body violently, as if drying himself. For Elmer this shaking was his way of moving from one frame of mind to another, the violent shake literally forcing out the old behaviour of play from his body, allowing for the new one of travelling and hunting to come in. He headed off.

Freya followed on quickly with Buster and Meg bringing up the rear. Freya was focused on the search ahead and the pups took advantage, spending the first few miles playing with each other as they moved, they couldn't help themselves, especially Buster.

The pups were 4 months old now and as they followed their parents the similarities were obvious, they looked just like little versions of them. Buster was black like Elmer and Meg was becoming grey like Freya, though she had no white patch on her chest or a kink in her tail. Buster was bold, big and strong, just like his father, and Meg was sleek and fast, just like her mother. Whether the pups would turn out like their parents in other ways would be determined by their other experiences as they went on their path through life.

As the family moved through their land Elmer and Freya would often stop to mark it, him with his usual high leg lift, her with a squat and little leg lift. Every few hundred yards they would slow for Elmer to do his thing, and often he would scrape the ground up vigorously afterwards. The pups watched every behaviour with great interest and concentration, briefly taking time to investigate their fathers marks, learning the ways of the wolf.

They had been travelling for a few hours, Elmer had slowed the pace a bit so the pups could keep up, when he suddenly slowed to a walk. Freya stopped, waiting for the pups to come up tight behind her. All three watched as Elmer walked slowly and deliberately ahead of them sniffing the ground and air as he went. He came to a small tree stump and stood there for a time smelling it and peering intensely past it, into the forest. Turning his head he gave a serious look back to Freya, and she stayed still with the pups.

Elmer left the almost path they were on and went into the forest, continually sniffing high and low as he moved. He hadn't gone far when he turned back to rejoin his family on the path. A quick look back to Freya and the pups, and he was on his way.

The pups could tell the difference in the movements of their parents now, both looked more focused and much busier, their heads moving much more frequently from side to side, as if looking for something. Now and then they would stop briefly to raise their noses high into the air. Elmer had come across the sign of a male lynx and he had been about recently.

The lynx was a large feline predator, a little smaller than Freya in size and a formidable hunter that regularly took prey much bigger than itself, adult Roe deer being their favourite. He would pose no real threat to Elmer and Freya but would easily be capable of taking one of the pups if they were to stray.

Freya moved back to the rear of the file. The pups watched and wondered why as she passed and took up her place behind them, both could see the extra seriousness in her ways. For the next mile or so Elmer kept a constant watch at the front of his family. He knew that these big cats mostly laid up during the day, and reassured himself that they were now past any possible danger. He speeded up slightly, Freya stayed at the back for a while.

The large male Lynx had watched the wolf family as they passed. In his short brown summer coat he lay perfectly camouflaged in his daytime lair just twenty yards from the path, bold enough to stay put as they filed closely by. Near to eighty pounds in weight, well muscled and in peak condition, these cats didn't come any bigger and there was little that really worried him in the forest. An excellent tree climber there was always a way of escaping larger predators, as long as he remained alert.

The big cat observed with interest the large black wolf at the head of his family, highly tuned feline senses telling him a story of a hugely powerful animal, alert and ready for anything when around his kin. He was the largest and most focused wolf the lynx had ever seen. In the future he would try to ensure their paths never crossed for something told him it might not end well for him if they did.

Elmer reached the area he was heading for, it was the place that he had come to with Orin, his father, when they had caught the two wild boar. Elmer had not hunted this area for a few weeks and was hoping the boar had got over their losses and settled down again. On his last visit there had been no dominant male with the group and he was hoping that this was still the case. Freya was keen to get on with the hunt. They would worry about finding a place to lie later.

CHAPTER 15

HOW QUICKLY THE TABLES CAN BE TURNED

Elmer headed off followed by Freya, with the pups close behind. They would cover the area using the animal paths to allow for quicker movement, continually scenting and listening for the wild boar as they moved. In the forest scenting was often the first sense to find something of interest, hearing and sight frequently being hampered by trees and dense foliage.

As they hunted Elmer always tried to head into or across the wind, this would allow any preys scent to be carried to them first, not the other way round. When they did find prey they often had to decide quickly on the way to handle it, drawing on their own experiences with the prey concerned and the environment in which they found it. If conditions allowed then Elmer and Freya, like most wolves, would observe the prey first, looking for any old, injured or young animals, and if none were present they would have to weigh up the risk of taking on a healthy animal against the possibility of injury, or worse.

If prey was to run then the wolf would almost always follow, it seemed to Elmer that this response was almost out of his control, a reflexive response to a fleeing animal. On a few occasions though, when they had time to assess possible prey before they ran, and had decided they were too fit, healthy, large or dangerous, they would let them go and just move on, looking for easier targets.

Elmer picked up the scent he was looking for, wild boar. Freya smelt it too and they headed towards it, the pups trailing eagerly behind. The families speed automatically increased for a while as the prospect of a possible hunt drew closer. Minutes later Elmer slowed again to a walk, starting to pick his way through the heavier foliage. Freya followed him close behind with the pups moving together at the rear. Sometimes one of the pups would stumble noisily in the long heavy foliage and receive a stern backward looking glance from Freya, both would look away as if to say, 'not me mum.'

For several minutes they slowly made their way through the greenness until some familiar sounds made them stop; the hustle and bustle of a nearby foraging wild boar family. They could not see them but Elmer knew they were not far away. The heavier summer brush and patches of high, dense grass would make it easier to get closer to them, but also harder to actually catch them once a chase started.

The boar were foraging in ground much thicker than when Elmer last hunted them with his father, maybe they were still conscious of their recent losses. The smaller boar would be harder to see, Elmer and Freya might not know exactly where they were until they came almost upon them. Elmer decided the best way to hunt them would be a fast, straight on attack, flushing them out and then chasing them down. They would have to be careful though, in such close brush the larger boar could appear seemingly from nowhere, they were fast, strong and well armed. Elmer drew some comfort from the fact that the dominant boar was not with the clan last time he hunted them.

Freya moved up beside Elmer and they moved purposefully forwards, side by side. Before they disappeared from view Freya glanced back to the pups, this was there sign to stop and stay, she didn't want them getting too close to these dangerous prey. Both pups settled down to try and watch proceedings, but the ground would make this nearly impossible; they would have to listen harder to try and learn more.

Much closer now, the adults separated and spread out. Moving slowly they were near enough now for their eyesight and hearing to come more into play. Something moved in a large thicket to Freya's right and as she advanced further a loud squeal erupted from it. She had been discovered.

The forest came instantly alive with the high pitched squeals of piglets and the loud, deep grunting of older boar, the entire clan tuned up and a temporary mayhem descended. Not sure of how many wolves were present or where they were the family of wild boar took off in all directions. These first moments of uncertainty were sometimes the time when prey would literally run straight into a waiting wolf, and today it was Freya's turn.

The top of the long woodland grass moved like a wave of water towards her as a panicking small boar ran blindly beneath it, she pounced and pinned the squealing piglet beneath the raft of dense grass, the thickness of it making it hard for her to actually get her jaws around it. Freya tried to hold the piglet and clear the grass above it at the same time so she could grab it; there it was. She was just about to clamp down on it when a large bush on the very edge of her vision erupted.

Enraged and ill tempered, the dominant male was only yards away and bearing down on her quickly. A ball of rock hard muscle almost twice her weight, he was heavily armed and being driven without fear by the flood of testosterone now surging through his body. The boar lowered his head just before impact, intending to drive upwards from underneath into the wolf's soft belly, where his three inch tusks would do major damage.

Freya had waited too long in an attempt to grab the piglet and run off with it. She winced and let out a loud cry as the boar smashed into her side. Freya rode up onto the top of his head and he came quickly to a halt, flicking his granite like appendage upwards with tremendous force; years of grubbing through rock hard ground for bulbs and tubers and fighting with other male boar had given the giant pig almost unrivalled power in his neck and shoulders, he could uproot tree stumps. Unable to do anything about it Freya was thrown through the air.

She landed awkwardly on top of a large bush, but it cushioned her just a little, and afforded her some immediate protection from the rampaging boar. Freya crouched in the centre of the bush as the boar tried his best to destroy the forest around her. Dazed and badly hurt she tried to take stock of her situation.

Amazingly, Freya's stomach had not been pierced by the boar's tusks in the first attack. She calmed herself down and things started to become a little clearer. Freya thought she could see a way out. The dominant boar was in a blind rage now, goring anything within reach and taking little notice of the wolf. Freya's cool tactical mind came back to her. She picked the right moment and made good her escape, leaving the boar to take it out on the forest.

Freya was in real pain. She returned to the pups, wanting to get them out of the immediate area. As she approached Freya tried her

93

best to move normally, hoping to hide the seriousness of her injuries from her pups, but two worried heads peered towards her; they knew something was wrong. She trotted over to them, giving them both a quick reassuring nudge and the look to follow her. Turning quickly she headed back to the path, her uneasy pups in tow.

Elmer had been taken well away from Freya as he pursued a juvenile boar. This medium sized wild pig would be a good meal. Elmer, focusing intently on his task, had heard but did not registered properly the sounds of the distant enraged boar. He eventually caught up with his prey, grabbing it by the rear end and pulling it to the ground. A long and sustained struggle followed, Elmer having to use all his strength and experience to eventually subdue the squealing youngster. Luckily for him the dominant Sow had smaller family to look after and had not answered the juvenile's cries.

The young boar weighed about fifty pounds and Elmer could just about carry it, but not for long. He wanted to get his prize back to his family and a place of safety so they could all eat together. As he made his way back Elmer could hear the ever louder grunting of a boar moving around the forest, he could tell it came from a large frustrated male and the sound of it put him on edge, so much so that he often dropped his kill to listen for it's whereabouts properly.

The boar was definitely coming his way. Elmer dropped his prize at his feet and stood tall above it, staring hard into the thick forest and brush ahead of him. He would not be persuaded to leave it easily. More long, deep and intense grunts reverberated around the forest, bouncing off the trees and the canopy, making the sound seem even more menacing. Elmer could hear the long undergrowth being trampled by the approaching boar and readied himself.

The boar burst out of the thick brush and kept coming, it didn't know the wolf was there yet. Just twenty yards away the giant wild pig stopped dead in his tracks. Elmer knew he was dealing with the clans dominant male. Both stared at each other, the boar paying little attention to his dead brethren lying at the wolf's feet. Elmer was outweighed by a third, both were well armed, the boar was stronger but the wolf faster. In a head on fight it would not go Elmer's way, the boar would be too strong and dangerous, he would have to use fight and flight tactics and hope the big male moved on, but he stood his ground for now.

The dominant boar could tell that the wolf standing before him now was different from the one he had seen off earlier, he knew this wolf would not give up easily and they stood there for just a few seconds, measuring each other up.

The huge pigs testosterone fuelled aggression of earlier was subsiding quickly. With no living members of his family in the immediate vicinity to protect, and being drawn by the distant cries of his females, he made up his mind to leave. He wouldn't go quietly though. A couple of deep, long, rumbling grunts were directed towards the wolf. Elmer prepared himself to move quickly, still not sure of the huge pigs intentions. The dominant male boar turned his body slightly away, took another long look at the big black wolf, then barrelled off at speed, smashing his way through a small bush that stood in his way.

Elmer felt a little relieved. He would have fought the boar, not to win but more for the well earned meal that lay before him. He could have left and came back later to claim his prize but he knew that boar and many others in the forest ate meat; it might not have been there for him to collect on his return. He picked the carcass up and carried it away, going as far as he could in one go before having to drop it, resting for just a minute then moving on, he too wanted to get out of the area. A few minutes later and he came to the place where they had left their pups. They were not there, but Elmer didn't worry, he knew that Freya had moved them. He followed their tracks.

Freya and the pups were not far away now. Elmer dropped his carcass and let out a few short, quiet woofs. A few seconds later he let out some more. In no time Elmer was being greeted by his excited pups rushing towards him, licking his mouth and nudging into him. Elmer watched Freya as she approached, his knowledgeable eyes telling him something was wrong with her, but she still pushed her head firmly into the side of his. Elmer went to push his head into her side but stopped quickly as he felt her pull away from him. She went away a little and laid down. Elmer quickly opened the tough carcass, then went over to reassure and lay beside her, he knew his mate had been badly injured. Together they watched as their pups fed on the young boar.

CHAPTER 16

SIGNS OF OTHERS

Freya had been trying to hide the real seriousness of her injuries but it was obvious to Elmer in many ways. Sometimes he could see the silent wince within her when she rose to her feet, and her tolerance of the pups, especially when they wanted some rough play, was much reduced. When Elmer approached her from her left side looking for physical contact she would pull away, he could see that she wanted to protect this area. He would try to make sure he only approached from the right side for now. Elmer hoped that whatever was wrong with her would fix itself. He spent most of the morning being around Freya, reassuring her with his strong but gentle ways, and she adored him for it.

Several of Freya's ribs had been fractured when the boar hit her. She had been lucky though, the broken ribs had not caused any damage to her internal organs and the boar's tusks had not gored her; a serious goring from a large male boar would often lead to death by disembowelment or later from infection. Over time the ribs would heal themselves but it would mean several weeks of pain and reduced capability for her. Freya might have been a sleek wolf but they came no tougher or resilient and she was not alone, the support of Elmer would make all the difference.

Elmer worried little that for the near future he would be the sole provider for his family. The pups were still too young to be of any real help to him in the hunt, they would more likely be a hindrance, but this was also an important time for the pup's development, they needed to come along on hunts to watch and learn. Elmer decided that for the next few days the family would put off their nomadic existence and stay in one place, giving Freya some time to start healing. He would leave the pups with Freya and head of alone to patrol their land and hunt. The pups might wonder what was happening at first but they would cope.

Two sets of young wolf eyes watched their father closely as he prepared to go off. Rising from his position next to Freya he moved slightly away and carried out his usual vigorous body shake. The pups could see the slight difference in their father's behaviour this morning, there was not the usual eye contact, physical exchanges and mutual excitement at the prospect of moving off, both sensed he did not want to be accompanied today.

Elmer trotted off alone. After just a hundred yards he stopped and looked back over his shoulder. Still within eyesight of his family he concentrated his gaze on the pups. Both pups sat bolt upright looking back towards him, Elmer could just make out their little bodies moving slightly from side to side in time with their hidden tails, an expectant look still on their faces. Even from that distance the pups could make out and understand the message conveyed in their fathers looks and body posture. Both slowly lay back down, Buster giving out a big long sigh; they would definitely be staying put today.

The steady pace of Elmer's travel was interrupted frequently as he stopped to mark the land or investigate something that his nose thought warranted it. Every few hundred yards he would leave his sign on prominent places, scratching the immediate ground up vigorously afterwards before moving on. The young boar he killed yesterday had been a decent meal, and unless he was lucky enough to come across an easy target on his travels any further hunting would be left for another day.

Like all pack leaders Elmer took this patrolling part of his life seriously. Driven by feelings from deep inside him, and from what he had learnt from watching his own father, he carried this behaviour out with great focus; to him it seemed to be one of the most important parts of his life.

He trotted along a small animal path, keeping his head at the same level as his back, it took him a little less effort to do this than to keep his head up high, when he did though come across something of interest he would stop and raise his head up high, to try and get some more information.

His nose brought him quickly to a halt. He stood tall, sniffing the air heavily both high and low, employing too his eyes and ears to scan the area before him. Elmer followed this new scent into the trees. The canopy here was dense and little light made its way through to the forest floor, there was some vegetation on the floor but it was much sparser than most of the forest, Elmer moved through it easily. His nose lead him on to a rotten old tree stump in a small depression, one that would have held water at other times of the year, the lingering smell of dampness was all around. There was another scent about this stump though, the one that had drawn him in her, he investigated it further.

Elmer's body started to stiffen in an almost uncontrollable reaction to the scent. Moving much slower now his nose worked hard to decipher the smells about. The sign was a few days old and it came from another male wolf, there were faint signs of other wolves about but only this one had marked. Elmer was close to the land that lay between his land and others, but this was the first time he had found some sign on their side. It was the breeding male of the much larger neighbouring pack.

He spent the next few minutes trying to eradicate and cover the intruder's marks with ones of his own. Large clods of earth, leaves and twigs flew through the air as he scrapped up the ground all around with powerful backward swipes of all four of his paws. He urinated frequently on top of any foreign marks he found and on obvious raised objects. Finally he laid some of his excrement in the centre of the area, a powerful message for any that might return.

Sure that he had left signs to make any intruders think again he returned to the path and went on his way, skirting along the edge of his territory for the next few miles, looking for any further sign of intruders. If any was found the area would get the same treatment.

It was almost dusk when Elmer got back to his family. Freya was stood waiting for him, the pups standing either side of her. Buster and Meg rushed forwards and excitedly ploughed into him, squealing and whining as they did so. Elmer acknowledged them with a few quick playful barges then walked over to Freya and gently but firmly pushed his head into the side of hers. She pushed back and reassuringly he could still feel the strength within her. Elmer would try to make sure he didn't communicate any worry about what he had found today, he would though, be extra vigilant when patrolling over the next few weeks. Elmer backed away from Freya to play with his pups.

Twenty minutes later Buster and Meg were flat out on their backs, almost lifeless, all four paws reaching for the sky, the only movement to be seen was the rising and falling of their deep little chests. Elmer hadn't known it but in between bouts of exploring the surrounding area they had also been playing hard with each other all day; their almost boundless energy now finally exhausted.

The night drew in dark and still. The moon was nearly full but the thick cloud cover let little of its light reach the ground. Elmer peered skywards, small areas of brightness appeared through the brakes in the clouds sending beams of light down to the ground, holding his attention. The late summer air carried a slight chill but Elmer ignored it as an inner warmth started building up within him.

He moved around quickly, looking for the right place, finding it and then settling down on his haunches into a sitting position. He slowly laid his head back into his shoulders as far as it would go, peering upwards for just a second, before closing his eyes tightly. The cool night air came instantly alive with his meaningful song.

Freya, ignoring her pain, jumped up and trotted over quickly to join him. She shuffled around at her partners side, trying to get comfortable, finally settling down on his right. She laid her own head back and with just a little tentativeness pushed out a howl. It didn't seem to cause her any real pain, so she used more power, and an equally beautiful, higher pitched howl, joined his.

The pups sprung up from their slumber and were quickly overtaken by their enthusiasm to join in. After a few exchanges of mutual barges and excitable growls they steadied themselves. Still standing they made several attempts of their own: little whines, squeals and broken howls intermingled with their parent's song. Buster and Meg could tell their efforts were falling short. Both looked at their parents and thought that sitting might have something to do with their success, they ran over and adopted squatting positions, Meg next to her mum and Buster next to his dad.

The harmonious howling of Elmer and Freya carried on for several minutes, occasionally accompanied by an almost successful one from the pups. Elmer was hoping that the vigorous marking that he done earlier combined with his family howling together now, would send an even stronger message to the neighbouring packs.

Other wolf ears were listening that night, they were several miles away in their own territory, but on this calm, still night, the family's howls travelled far and told the hearers much.

CHAPTER 17

THE LYNX

It had been a week since Elmer found the intruders sign on their land. He had been patrolling vigorously all that time and had found no new marks to worry him. More than the normal amount of howling sessions had been instigated recently, to send a message to others, but like most wolves, he also just loved to howl.

Elmer had been keeping his family well fed but he could see that it was now time for them to get back to their nomadic ways. Freya and the pups were getting irritable and frustrated and they also needed to carry on the pups schooling.

Freya was still in some pain whenever she first got up to move but once moving it was bearable for her, she did though have some doubts about how she would perform if hunting a strong prey animal. Elmer somehow knew her thoughts and told himself that he would try to ensure any hunting done in the near future would be something that he could do alone, that would not require Freya to get involved. He knew this might not be so easy though, his partner loved to hunt and once caught up in it there would be no stopping her. Elmer made his mind up that if Freya really wanted to hunt then she must feel ready too. He would let her do her own thing.

Elmer was lying on his side with Freya to his right and the pups to his left. Buster lay on his side too, with Meg sprawled across the rear half of his body, her head nestled into his back. Buster was thinking what this morning might hold for them, hoping to get back out into their territory, to follow his parents and learn from their every move.

None of the family was really asleep, and all eyes fell on Elmer as he stretched his whole body outwards then rolled onto his back, wriggling violently. He rose to his feet and as he did so his large amber eyes fell quickly in turn on each member of his family. The look he gave them was the one they had all been waiting for.

Buster sprang instantly to his feet throwing his sister from his back and depositing her unceremoniously on the forest floor. Her top lip briefly curled back, exposing her bright white teeth and showing her annoyance, but Buster didn't even see it, he was already far to excited. Freya rose less quickly to her feet, but she too was eager to get on the move, stepping over sideways to her partner she pushed her head firmly into his unmoving side, running her head along his body, tail to head. As she reached Elmer's head he turned and nuzzled her affectionately.

Both pups came over to join in, pushing into their parents bodies. Freya felt a tinge of pain but tried not to show it. The pups started to get even more excited, the squeals and whines of anticipation getting louder, and the adults couldn't help but get caught up in it. The next few minutes were taken up with bouts of ever louder vocalisations and boisterous play moves by Elmer and the pups, Freya stood off just a little. They hadn't been out as a family for a few days and the bottled up feelings of frustration were now coming out.

Elmer pulled away from his excited family, a look of seriousness setting in about him. He trotted a short distance away, stopped and carried out his usual vigorous body shake. It was time to go. Before leaving Elmer left his mark at the base of the towering beech tree that stood over where they had lain that night. Freya noticed him scraping up the ground afterwards with much more vigour and for longer than he normally would. She followed him over to the tree and as he moved away she left her own sign on the other side of it; it seemed to her that an extra strong message was required this morning, she duly backed up her partner. Buster and Meg, though still young pups, had also noticed the forcefulness in their father's marking behaviour, and if not truly excited about the prospect of moving off today, might have thought more of it.

Elmer set off at a pace slightly slower than normal, followed closely by Freya. The first few minutes were a bit painful for her but things eased of greatly as she got into her stride. The pups brought up the rear, Meg in front. Buster kept close to his sister for the first few miles, so he could clout her rear end with one of his front paws, it was fun to him, but to her it was annoying. He gave up on it when he noticed Freya's stern backward glance boring into him.

Buster padded along happily at the back, soaking up the sights and smells of their land all around, bold and fearless he would follow his parents anywhere they asked him to go and couldn't wait to get older, to be able to help feed and protect his family, to be like his father; he knew he had to get bigger and learn much more, but truly relished the thought of it.

Meg was getting more like her mother, not just physically but behaviourally too, approaching all things with much more seriousness than her brother. She wanted to be like her mother, a fast skilful hunter, but she also had the greatest admiration for her father. Lately Meg could see her father's ways coming out in her brother. Buster might play the fool sometimes but he was fearless and bold, just like their father, Meg had no doubts that he would always be there for them.

A strong scent flooded Elmer's nose, stopping him dead. Raising his head high and sniffing deeply he searched for more clues. Freya had responded too, her head also held high and looking as intense as Elmer. Buster and Meg stood still and eagerly behind them, waving their noses about, waiting expectantly for their parent's response.

Elmer left the main path and headed off slowly into the trees. Freya stayed on the track with the pups, that had now moved up beside her. Buster, knowing now that it was not just possible prey that had stopped them, moved slightly forward taking up a position just in front of Freya and Meg; young though he was he already thought to protect them.

Elmer moved slowly and deliberately, picking his way through the thick undergrowth while trying to be as quiet as possible. The scent that had brought him into the trees was one of blood, maybe from another hunters kill. Wolves were not averse to taking kills of other predators and this was well within his territory, but he would have to be careful, at times there was a much bigger predator to be found in these woods. As he closed a second scent filtered its way in, causing him to stop and scan the area ahead of him with even more purpose.

The other scent now became clear to him, it was one he had come across recently. He relaxed just a little for he now knew what it was before him; a few weeks earlier the family had come across the scent of a large male lynx and it was this same scent that now coursed through his nostrils.

Using it's stealthy ambush tactics the big lynx had taken down a roe deer doe almost the same size as himself. It was a good meal that would normally feed him for many days, but he didn't want to be killed over it. One on one with a smaller wolf the lynx could well make a fight of it, but this Lynx had seen Elmer and his family before.

Elmer slowly approached the carcass, he had been moving quietly and carefully but the Lynx knew he was coming and had retreated a safe distance to watch his usurper approach. Not much of the deer had been eaten and Elmer knew the owner was probably watching him from afar. He stood over it, to make his claim, at the same time scouring the surrounding woods for any sign of the Lynx.

The large male cat was not far away and becoming more eager to get going. He took one last look at his kill and the big black wolf before him, then melted backwards into the greenness, moving downwind his well furred paws gave him almost silent footfall. He was gone.

The carcass was just a little too heavy to carry, so Elmer made an effort to drag it back towards his family. The Lynx had left but still he did not like the thought of having his pups in the vicinity of such an accomplished killer. The ground cover was making hard work of moving the carcass, so Elmer made up his mind to bring his family to the kill: he would watch over them closely. Leaving the carcass Elmer quickly covered the ground back to his waiting family. Emerging onto the path he gave them a quick look that said, 'follow me,' and spun back round again. Freya and the pups were instantly on his heels.

As they approached the carcass the pups became excited and speeded up to get to it. Elmer carried on a few yards past it and stood still scanning the ground all around. Freya stopped short of the carcass and turned to scan the ground behind her, she had scented the possible danger also and would keep guard with Elmer as the pups fed. The pups too had also smelt the Lynx but thoughts of food had prevailed and anyway their parents were with them. The meal was a decent one and there would be plenty to go round. The familiar raven had already appeared on the scene and others were dropping in but they wouldn't get much of a look in today; Freya would make sure of that.

Later, the pups had eaten their fill and laid down a short distance from the carcass, putting their well rounded bellies on show. Elmer and Freya now moved in to eat their share, they were not worried about the Lynx now, he was well gone, both enjoyed the rewards of the big cat's hard work. There was enough meat here for another feed and Freya would stay close to it to keep the scavengers away, a further day's free food would mean more rest for her and she could do with that at the moment.

Dusk was soon upon them and the good fortune of the day had lifted the spirits of the whole family. After a few hours to let the meal digest Elmer moved away a little and got into a comfortable sitting position. Watched by Freya he laid his head back, closed his eyes, and let out his long and beautiful howl, pure pleasure etched into his face. As always Elmer's howling brought an almost instant reaction from the pups. Buster body checked his smaller sister almost knocking her over and she retaliated with a quick growling attack to the back of his head. Buster knew that it was nothing serious and took a minute to have a go back. While the pups worked themselves up into a frenzy Freya went over and took her place beside Elmer, she tilted her head skywards, her eyes closed and the early night time air filled with the couple's haunting song.

Buster barged his sister off him now, that was enough play fighting, he wanted to howl too and trotted over, sitting down on his little haunches beside his father, he tried his best. Not wanting to be left out Meg dashed over to take her place beside her big brother, joining him in the quest for the perfect howl.

Elmer and Freya howled together for several minutes then almost together they stopped. Meg had already stopped trying but Buster was so enthralled in his efforts to howl that for a second or two he had not noticed his parents had finished, his broken little howls and whines pierced the air alone. All the family were captivated.

CHAPTER 18

LIVING WITH RAVENS

All that remained of the roe deer carcass killed by the Lynx was some fur and bones that the ravens and crows were now fighting over. Freya had made sure that little of real worth was left for them but still the large black birds squabbled, pecked and fenced with their dagger like beaks; it was in their nature to.

Elmer had moved his family off early this morning, today would be a day for patrolling their land and refreshing the signs of their residency, they would cover a fair amount of ground but it would be easy travelling and still a rest of sorts for Freya.

The large familiar raven had left his kind behind to fight over the scraps, and hopped almost silently from tree to tree following his wolf family. The raven spent much time following Elmer and his pack. Among the brightest and longest lived of birds this raven had studied and learnt the behaviours associated with the ways of the wolf, especially Elmer. The clever bird knew that hunting was not on the mind of this wolf today but he would still follow them anyway. The wolf was an opportunist hunter and on occasion when travelling might come across an unexpected meal that it could not pass by, the end result sometimes being a feed for the more persistent bird.

As Elmer moved he often kept an eye on the treetops and the sky when he could see it. He too had learnt some things, that these clever black birds, who regularly followed them and appeared from nowhere at their kills, were well tuned into the environment and the ways of many of the animals that lived in it. On more than one occasion Elmer had followed the signs of descending ravens and crows to a carcass, they were experts at finding them, and if they were actually on the carcass eating it then whatever might have killed the animal may not be close by. Elmer always approached any carcass with care though.

Sometimes an animal may just have died of natural causes and not predation. On these occasions when such an animal was found by the ravens they might be unable to get through the tough hide. The intelligent birds would call out aloud, making a fuss to attract a predator, and lead them to it so they could open it for them, allowing all to have a feed. Elmer had done this before himself; truly one relying on the other.

Elmer had no real problem with the ravens, to him it was always seemed a two way affair, each benefited from the other. The raven did indeed take food from the wolfs table, but mostly it was only in times of plenty. In harsher times Elmer and his family would bury left over food out of the ravens reach, or simply stay near the carcass to guard it until all that they wanted from it had been consumed. Freya was good at this, she hated the ravens and other scavengers, and could see no good in them like Elmer. Because of her vigilance the ravens and their kind took less from their kills than from other wolves.

The ravens also had another benefit though, informing others of danger. On occasion the ravens, sat high in their loftier perches, would forewarn the wolf about the approach of a threat with their raucous warning calls, Elmer now recognized these warnings and always took notice of them.

It was early afternoon by the time the raven gave up on following his wolf family, flying off to find other pickings. Elmer watched him leave, his healthy dark black feathers shining brightly as they reflected the afternoon sunlight. The birds direct and purposeful flight told the knowing wolf he wouldn't be back today. Freya paid little attention to the comings and goings of the raven, she only showed interest in them when they were eating her kill. Elmer sometimes wondered about this side of Freya, it seemed to him that the raven had always been a part of the wolf's life, that they were somehow connected.

Buster and Meg always watched with great interest the behaviour of their parents as they patrolled and marked their land. Every time one or both of their parents marked something they would wander over to have a quick sniff, before running to catch up. When one of their parents showed a more intense interest in anything the pups would wait for them to move on then run over and investigate it for themselves, to try and work out why. Life was a continual learning

107

curve for the pups and they were seemingly inexhaustible in their enthusiasm to observe and learn: as though their lives depended on it.

All wolf pups were born with certain traits and behaviours already in place, these came courtesy of evolution and a mix of their family genes, but how a wolf eventually turned out would be shaped by the learning from their parents and the environment in which all this took place. Buster and Meg would learn to hunt the same way as their parents did, which in some cases might be different to how other wolves might do it. The young wolf was always learning, but those first weeks and months spent watching their parents and interacting with the environment, would mould them.

The social way of the wolf had to be learnt too, this had started at day one when with reflex actions they had jostled for a place on Freya's teats. Buster and Meg were already well versed in the body language of the wolf, much could be communicated from just a look or the positioning of a certain part of the body; but there was always more to learn.

Dusk was falling, the moon was full and the sky clear and bright, autumn was around the corner and you could feel it in the chill that now descended. Freya searched for a place to lie. The moonlight was particularly bright tonight and would give most prey an advantage, they had eaten well recently so they would just relax tonight. Freya found a spot beneath a large old oak tree, one of the many like this that were scattered throughout their land, these massive trees seemed to harbour a feeling of security within her when she lay under them.

She circled the large trunk finding a place that best afforded her protection from the chilly breeze, using it as a natural wind break, she then scraped up some of the forest litter into a small pile and settled down to watch her young family play.

Elmer looked hard at both the pups then went down into a deep play bow. Buster reacted instantly, charging flat out at his father. Meg would let Buster get stuck in and take most of their fathers attention before piling in herself. Playful growls erupted from father and son as Buster jumped on his fathers back. Elmer purposefully fell over sideways to let Buster think he had done it and Buster doubled his efforts, thinking he had actually taken his mighty father down.

Meg came in now and grabbed Elmer's tail, tugging on it and growling loudly. Elmer rolled over quickly and Buster was sent sprawling away, giving him time to grab Meg. He pinned her by her midsection with one of his huge paws and gnawed playfully on one of her back legs, she turned her head backwards to try and chew on the paw that pinned her, growling and wriggling violently, struggling in vain to escape her fathers grip.

Buster could see her plight and for a second enjoyed watching it, but then dashed over to leap again onto his fathers back, proceeding to gnaw vigorously on one ear then the other. Busters attack made good Meg's escape, she moved quickly away and after getting her bearings rushed back in and pounced up onto her father's back with Buster.

Both pups growled deeply as they scrambled for grip on their fathers back. Elmer shot off then planted all four feet firmly into the ground bringing himself to an abrupt halt, the force of it depositing both pups over his head into a heap at his feet.

Sporadic bouts of rough play carried on for some time, the doting father never getting too rough with them. He could feel the strength increasing within his pups and loved it; not just the play but the good feeling that came from having his own, fit, strong and healthy pups.

All the family slept well that night, the pups because they were tired, Elmer because he was happy and Freya because she needed to, there was still some healing to be done.

The morning arrived and was accompanied by a cool wet mist that hung low over the ground. The oak tree, still quite heavy in foliage, had done its job and kept the family dry, a circular ring of wetness could be seen spreading outwards on the forest floor from the edge of the trees natural umbrella above them.

Elmer raised himself up, bringing little murmurs of objection from the dozing pups beside him. He walked slowly over to a nearby fallen birch tree to leave his mark, a quick look around saw the familiar raven sitting quietly above him, watching back. Elmer returned to his dozing family and lay back down.

CHAPTER 19

THE BEAR

It had been four weeks now since Freya was injured by the wild boar, her pain had eased a lot. Elmer could see his partners effortless and flowing movement returning.

This morning was cold and damp. A thick mist carpeted the ground and all had been covered in a heavy dew. More mornings were like this now and Elmer knew it would not be long before the trees would start to shed their leaves and the days get much colder. Winter was still a fair way off yet though, and the family for now, enjoyed these times of easy movement.

The pups returned from some play, both dripping wet from rolling together in the soaking grass. Buster came over and stood beside Freya, shaking himself violently to throw the worst of the water from his back. Freya received an unwelcome shower and gave Buster the look, he quickly trotted off and around to the far side of his resting father, flopping on him heavily. The wetness didn't bother Elmer as he pinned his son to the ground then let him up and took off after him. Meg lay beside her mother and both watched father and son as they played.

It was time to go. Elmer put a stop to the play and they all prepared to leave. The family quickly became excited, the forest filling with the usual, excitable, high pitched whines and squeals, Buster almost howling as he was taken over by his enthusiasm. Elmer had no real plan for today, it would be one to patrol, like many other days, but if they happened on something of interest, then all could change.

Elmer took the lead with Freya close behind him, usually Buster brought up the rear, more so he could annoyingly bother his sister as they moved, but today he seemed extra excited and was up behind his mother. Meg brought up the rear. Meg was more confident now but still not as bold as her big brother; she was fine now though with being at the rear on her own.

An hour later and the family were moving steadily along the small path that ran beside the river on one side of their land. All the family recognized the area they were moving through. It was their old den site. Elmer slowed to smell and mark the area. Freya approached the remains of her first den, sniffing heavily the area around it. The pups were not far behind her and both joined their mother, slowly covering the ground, heads down and sniffing hard, looking for something. Buster wandered off to find the spot where he last lay with their little sister. Seconds later he was under that same oak tree, sniffing all around it.

Many weeks had passed since she was there, time and weather had all but removed her scent but Buster was sure he could smell something. He whined gently and pushed his nose through the dirt. Meg joined him and nudged into his side, reassuring him, before putting her own nose to the ground. Freya arrived now and joined her pups, scenting the small mound and nudging into them.

It was a few minutes before Elmer found them. He had been off on a short journey of his own, to the place where he had finally hidden her little body. They all stayed in the area for a few more minutes before Elmer gave the signs to move off again. Buster and Meg stayed for just a moment to sniff their old home further, before running to catch up their parents.

They had travelled for about an hour from their old den site when Elmer brought them to a standstill. Freya had smelt it too. The scent of blood filled the air. Freya turned her head back towards the pups to see them both stood still, heads held high, scenting the air too. They moved off again staying on the path for now, it was going the way Elmer wanted to go and he speeded up slightly. The sound of feeding and bickering ravens began to reach Elmer's ears. He moved faster.

It sounded like the ravens were in a bit of a feeding frenzy, this usually meant no predators were nearby, but he would still go carefully when he got closer. The scent was strong now, not just blood but also the scent of deer, Red deer.

Sure now that a red deer carcass lay ahead of them Elmer slowed and moved more deliberately; it may have been hunted and if this was the case it must have been by a predator of at least their match. Elmer scented the air and the ground hard as he moved forwards, another scent now began filtering its way into Elmer's nose. It was a bear, a brown bear.

Brown bears were a lot bigger than their black cousins and much more aggressive. Fights between wolves and brown bears nearly always came out in the bears favour. Elmer looked back to Freya and she stopped firm with the pups up tightly behind her. Buster made a slight movement forwards, he wanted to join his father, but Freya willed him still with her steely gaze.

Elmer left the path and moved forwards, picking carefully where to place his paws as he went, it was still a fair distance to the carcass. The ravens and crows were bragging ever louder now, knowing the large wolf was approaching. As Elmer emerged from cover the flying scavengers raised up as one into the trees, revealing a half eaten Red deer stag carcass. He moved closer, all his senses straining to pierce the surrounding area as he went, the scent of bear was strong. Almost up to the carcass he stopped still and stared hard at it. Elmer could see it was the powerful old stag that had nearly taken his own life just weeks before; he became even more on edge.

He stood above the dead stag, casting his experienced predators eyes over it. Pawing and then pulling hard on the deer's antlers he could feel no resistance, it's neck had been broken. Not many bears were capable of killing a large stag in this way, with one swipe of it's mighty paw. Elmer knew it was the work of a powerful and experienced bear. He stepped over the carcass and moved forwards to scan the area to the front, spending the next few minutes reassuring himself that it was safe to bring his family in. Satisfied all was well he returned quickly to his waiting family and brought them in.

The pups as usual needed no prompting and descended quickly on the carcass while Elmer stood guard. It was a large beast with still plenty to go round, Freya joined the pups to feed. Several minutes later, alert and still tense, Elmer left his position as guardian to join his family in the free feast.

Luck had lead them again to an easy meal but knowing that the owner of this kill could return at any time they bolted it down as quickly as they could. Elmer sensed that this bear would be one that could not be turned away.

It took only twenty minutes for the whole family to eat their fill, normally they would stay close to a kill, but Elmer decided they would move away from it tonight, then come back tomorrow. If it was still safe they would have another day feeding on it then move on.

The next morning was brighter and colder. Elmer raised his family early from their slumber beneath one of the forests large oak trees, they would head straight for the carcass and hopefully another easy meal. They moved quickly to the bears kill only slowing when close. Elmer moved ahead alone and straight away he knew something was different. He carried on moving forwards his nose and ears having already told him that something else was on the kill; he knew what it was.

Elmer had moved into the wind so stealthily that he was almost on the carcass before the ever vigilant ravens in the trees above gave him away. Surprise now gone he rushed forwards into the small clearing in which the kill laid.

Two large juvenile male boar were on the carcass enjoying some meat, a rare treat for them, and one they relished when they came across it. Both had seen the wolf but carried on eating until the smaller of them lost his courage and took off. The remaining boar was bigger but Elmer had seen off boar this size before. There was still plenty of meat left on the carcass for him and his family and he quickly decided he would scare him off, then fetch Freya and the pups.

The remaining boar didn't want to give up his meal without a fight, he may have been a juvenile but was still capable of doing some serious damage if Elmer got it wrong. Elmer knew he might have to get physical to make him leave. The two watched each other closely, waiting for one to make their move, just then, Freya rushed into the arena. Bristling and snarling she took her place beside her partner. It was all that was needed, the boar turned quickly and snorting loudly barrelled of through the undergrowth.

The pups were not far behind their mother. Buster burst into the clearing wanting to do his bit. The boar had already gone but still he stalked around the carcass looking for it, staying alert for a minute or two, just in case the boar returned. After convincing himself that the threat was gone he turned to join his sister on the carcass. Elmer and Freya had watched the whole scenario with interest, both could plainly see the braveness within their young son. The whole family settled and started to feed quickly.

Elmer raised his head quickly from their meal, a far off look of concentration etched instantly into his face; he had heard something. He jumped across the carcass with one bound and took a few stiff, slow steps, towards the noise. The rest of the family stopped eating now and stood up. The distant snapping of twigs and branches could be easily heard as a large animal moved quickly their way. The forest temporarily fell quiet as the unseen animal stopped its charge, then came bursting back into life again, the air filling with a long deep roar, from an angry brown bear.

Elmer and Freya gauged from the depth of the sound and it's lasting power that this bear was large and meant business. Elmer retreated back to his family, if they had been without the pups he might have waited to see the opposition but he thought better of it. In more open land they might have an advantage with room to manoeuvre around the bear but in this heavily wooded area the bear would have the edge, one slip or mistake might well lead to death. Freya moved away from the approaching threat followed closely by the pups. Buster kept looking around for his father to make sure he was following. Elmer gave Buster a look that said, 'get a move on,' and he did.

Elmer followed his family for a short distance then stopped and turned back towards the bear, he could just make out the carcass still and was intrigued to see the opposition for himself. He glanced back over his shoulder towards his fast disappearing family; they were safe. He would wait to see this bear.

The bear was on the move again, with a slight downhill run towards it's kill he was moving fast, Elmer could hear the forest plants being smashed, trampled and pushed aside. The bear burst into the tiny clearing, roaring loudly as it did so. Quickly he straddled the carcass, roaring again in the direction of the departing wolves. Elmer was glad that they had not made a stand today, this bear was huge and very aggressive. Some bears were more combative towards wolves than others and this was surely one such bear. Elmer sensed though that something above the normal was driving this bear. He was right.

Six years earlier, when this bear was a cub, still with his mother and sister, they had wandered into the den area of a large wolf pack. His mother had seriously under estimated the size and aggression of the pack and in the ensuing fight his sister was mortally wounded and he badly injured, saved only by the tenacity and courage of his mother; she killed two wolves in the fight. He had never forgotten this incident and now as a huge male in his prime would go out of his way to fight wolves.

Elmer turned and moved off quickly to catch up with his family, if this large predator had decided to spend some time in their territory he would have to be even more vigilant.

That evening the family spent lots of time renewing and strengthening the bonds between them with mutual shows of love and affection, even Freya seemed to take great pleasure in it. Meg fell asleep with Buster lying heavily on top of her, one of his large paws placed squarely on her head, to any others it would have looked like a position of dominance but for Buster it was really the opposite; she was his sister and he would always protect her from any threat.

Elmer dozed off but sleep was hard to come by tonight. The days events were worrying him.

CHAPTER 20

DANGER IS NEVER FAR AWAY

Autumn was taking hold, a carpet of red and brown was starting to lay itself across the forest floor as the trees throughout their land slowly lost their leaves. Most mornings now had a deep chill to them but one that the wolf still easily felt comfortable in. Occasionally the sun would put in an appearance and the soft light would cover all in a strange glow. If you were lucky enough to find a sheltered position with the suns rays upon you then some warmth could still be felt.

Buster found himself in such a position this morning. Laying on the protected downwind side of a large tree, a strong beam of autumn sunlight had found its way down to him and as the sun moved slowly across the sky the beam of warmth moved slowly down his body. Buster laid there contentedly soaking it up. Yards away Meg was stirring. Buster followed her movements with his wandering blue eyes, hoping she would not come over to him, so he could carry on enjoying his bit of sun.

His wish was not granted. A now wide awake Meg could see her brother enjoying the moment and purposefully went over to spoil it. Buster raised his top lip and growled at her as she approached but she ignored him and piled in. His little moment of bliss now over Buster sprang up, barging into Meg's side and sending her sprawling, he would show his sister who was really the boss.

For the next few minutes Buster made a point of demonstrating to his sister how strong he really was as he knocked her over and pinned her for longer than he normally did. Meg could tell she had really annoyed him and knew he wanted to prove a point so she put up little resistance, so he would give up quicker; eventually he let her up and they both trotted over to Elmer and Freya.

It had been two months since Freya's injury and testament to her own strong nature and Elmer's care she was back to her old self again. Buster knew his mum was better and he didn't hold back as he ploughed into her. He might have been bigger than her now but his inexperience still showed against his mother as she easily turned the tables on him, rolling him over and mouthing the back of his head. She pinned him for a second but knew he had let her do it for he was already much stronger than her.

Seven months old now the pups were still not fully grown but both, especially Buster, could be taken for an adult at a distance. Meg was now three quarters the size of her mother and had developed a speed to almost match her. Buster was almost as tall as Elmer, he still had a little more growing to do and some size to put on but both Elmer and Freya knew there would not be much between them when he was an adult. Buster held all his family in great regard but felt that little something extra for his father.

Elmer had been right about Buster's eyes staying blue, they had not turned to the golden yellow colour of most adult wolves and he now looked deeply into them. Buster had finished his bout of play with his mother and approached his father, lowering his body slightly as a sign of respect and licking his fathers face as he pushed into his side. Elmer returned his son's advances and a little battle of strength followed, the wolf father revelling in the feelings within him as he playfully wrestled with his powerful young son. Buster felt just as good.

As Meg had got older she didn't play as much as her brother, just weeks before a ruff and tumble was always a welcome proposition and she had actively sort it out, but lately she seemed more serious. She took after her mother in many ways and she now laid beside her, watching Buster lose his wrestling match with his father. Had it been Meg losing a wrestling match Buster would have come over to help her but she left him to it.

Elmer now had his serious play head on. He may have been the packs breeding male but when in this mood the pup within him often took over. He trotted purposefully over to Freya and Meg, all the time being constantly head butted in the rear by Buster who trotted beside him. Buster was trying in vain to keep his fathers attention just on him, so he could play with him alone some more, but Elmer wanted to bring the rest of his family into it. Mother and daughter knew what was coming as the visibly excited Elmer increased his speed and crashed down between them; even in his excited state though, Elmer made sure he didn't drop his whole weight onto his partner.

Better to play with everyone than not at all, Buster thought, he followed his father and piled in, just a bit too heavily, into Meg. She growled loudly and retaliated by grabbing one of Buster's back legs in her mouth, tugging on it just a little too hard. Buster pulled his leg free and using his greater strength and weight rolled her over and pinned her again by her middle, he knew this always made her really mad and he enjoyed watching her squirm and growl beneath him. Elmer was rolling around with Freya, he still held back just a little bit as they pushed and pulled on each other, short excitable growls coming from them both.

Meg was getting wild now, and Buster let her up, he could see the anger in her piercing narrowed eyes and stiff poker like body as she ran at him snapping away with her front teeth as if trying to catch a fly. He turned and shot off, an infuriated Meg biting madly at his heels. Buster was enjoying the whole affair.

Elmer and Freya were temporarily oblivious to their pup's antics as they rolled around beside each other, the mood gradually turning from one of serious play to one of mutual affection. Buster and Meg charged off and disappeared into the forest.

The pups had travelled a fair distance from their parents, Meg's anger melting away to be replaced by some urges of play. She caught Buster's back leg, tripping him, and following him down. They both rolled around for a few seconds before Buster jumped back up. He pushed into his sister with his head, employing powerful neck and shoulder muscles to smudge her along the ground. Both young wolves growled loudly as they tried to get one over on the other, it might have been play but there was always that little bit of competition between them. Buster grabbed his sister by the back of the neck in a playful move, ready to try and pin her down, but then suddenly let go again. An unpleasant feeling had forced its way into his head: something was watching them.

Buster moved quickly into a stiff, aggressive, but also defensive stance, the speed and suddenness of his movements snapping Meg out of her own play mode too. Standing tall and unmoving his back bristled as he directed deep meaningful growls at a large group of thick bushes a short distance in front of them. He inched forwards slightly to take up a position just in front of Meg and stood his ground. Memories of a large fox that almost took his life when he was much younger flashed into his mind; but he was sure this was no fox.

Meg was starting to become worried now, backing up a little further behind her big brother. Her first warning barks were loud and sharp, they travelled quickly and easily back to their parents and hit Elmer's ears like a blow from one of his own sons large paws. He exploded up from his laying position and with Freya close behind sprinted towards the pups.

The giant brown bear had been resting in the clump of bushes. He had heard the wolves much earlier and decided not to move in the hope they might come much closer and give him a better chance of killing one. This was unusual behaviour, but this bear was an accomplished wolf killer. The bear knew now that surprise was lost and prepared to rush his adversaries, hoping one of them might stand to fight him, allowing him a chance of using his powerful swipe to bring them down.

Elmer and Freya entered the small clearing, Elmer immediately took up a position in front of Buster, closest to the still unseen threat. With four wolves before him the bear now pushed out of the thick bush into the open, he wanted to see his foe clearly before battle commenced. As soon as Elmer saw the bear he knew it was the one whose kill they had eaten from just weeks before.

The bear stood up on his back legs to emphasise his size and roared with a power that even Elmer took notice of. There was no den or kill to protect and the pups were fast enough to escape now, Elmer pondered quickly what his actions would be. The whole family knew they could not risk getting too close to the front of this bear, the ground around was reasonably open and afforded them an advantage with their quicker reactions but one slip would almost certainly end badly.

Buster and Meg were still too young and inexperienced to face such a foe and Elmer decided that harassing the bear would do little good. Better to move away and live to fight another day. Freya seemed to read Elmer's mind and ushered the pups away, she had to physically nudge Buster to get him moving. Elmer stood his ground for now giving his family time to move off.

The bear was back down on all fours, a deep grumble burbling from his throat as he smacked his lips and moved slowly around Elmer. Both watched each other closely. The bear was huge, powerful and angry.

Not far from denning for the winter the big brown bear had been eating well to pile on more fat to survive the forthcoming months underground, he was naturally at his heaviest, probably four times Elmer's weight and much stronger. The largest wolf this bear had ever seen stood before him but he had no fear of him. Elmer sensed this and it made him uneasy; most bears would show some sort of anxiety about taking on a wolf pack with such large members, not this one though.

When they wanted to bears could move deceptively quickly over a short distance, Elmer would make sure he didn't get too close. He backed up slowly, all the time growling and baring his teeth as he moved. The bear advanced, his huge size making his body sway from side to side, small dark eyes fixed on the wolf: Elmer could see plainly the anger and look of contempt within them.

Elmer thought about his family, they should have moved far enough away now. He turned quickly to make good his escape. The bear charged forwards as the wolf turned, roaring loudly, hoping that this might make him panic, force a mistake, a trip or a stumble; but Elmer was sure-footed as he sprinted away.

The bear followed the lone wolf, his passion for fighting them, driving him on. Elmer was well in front, he stopped for a while and watched behind him, the distant sounds of fallen branches snapping under the bears weight told him he was still coming. Elmer changed his direction, leading him away from the tracks of his family. Other bears would normally give up quickly when chasing a faster wolf but this one still tracked him, following from a distance. Elmer headed for the river. A bears sense of smell was exceptional, even better than that of a wolfs, so he decided to move along the bank of the river as fast as he could, until sure the bear had given up, then make his way back to his family.

Freya and the pups were now far away, she had brought them to a spot on the edge of the forest, the meadowland was close by and if the bear did turn up they could go out into it; the open space and room to move would give them a good advantage. Meg sought reassurance from Freya while Buster stood tall scanning the forest for his father and the bear, he had wanted to help his father but knew he didn't have the experience yet.

Elmer was moving up the river on the opposite side of the land from his waiting family. He entered the water several times to try and lose the bear, sometimes swimming, sometimes paddling, but he knew that distance would be his best tactic.

It had been several hours now and Elmer reassured himself that the bear would no longer be on his trail. He headed inwards to some slightly higher land in the centre of their territory. By the time he reached it the light was starting to fade, the evening air cold and still. Elmer thought about his family, waiting for him elsewhere in their territory. Sitting back on his powerful haunches he listened intently, tuning in to all around him. He was totally alone, all was quiet, nothing stirred. Elmer laid back his huge head, closed his eyes and reached deep down into the depths of his inner being, and the still night air came alive with his powerful song. Two long howls swept out across the land, the second much stronger and louder than the first. All fell quiet.

Elmer waited, motionless and expectant. Just seconds later an answer came to his calls. Elmer stood up, tall and erect, turning his head their way. He was immediately bolstered up by the great comfort that accompanied hearing the howls of his partner, and the broken cries of his pups. He knew where they were now, that they were safe, and immediately set off towards them. Elmer moved much faster than his normal trot, he had many miles to cover but it would not take him long. Freya knew her partner would be coming, she and the pups laid beside each other, waiting and listening for his arrival.

Buster was the first to hear something and his head spun round towards it. Elmer was approaching downwind and his family could not smell him. Freya and Meg came up beside Buster, all of them staring in the direction of the approaching noises, not sure yet if it was Elmer. Freya was almost certain the approaching animal was not the bear, the noises would have been much greater from such a large animal, but still she was a little troubled. Buster sensed his mothers worry and moved himself forwards slightly: if need be, he would do his bit.

Elmer knew his family might be anxious about his return, knowing he was moving into the wind he woofed loudly to reassure them. Buster was the first to move, rushing forwards to greet his father with a barrage of licks and nudges. Freya and Meg were right behind him and the whole family celebrated their reunion, nudging and rubbing against each other as whines, squeals and little howls of joy filled the night air.

Elmer had not been gone long but the circumstances had made it serious.

CHAPTER 21

WINTER IS COMING

It had been a month now since the families tangle with the massive, aggressive bear. Elmer had been extra vigilant patrolling and marking his territory, and was quite sure he had moved on to another's land. Elmer knew the bear would be denning for the winter soon and hoped he would do so far from their home, emerging in the spring, aggressive and hungry, in someone else's land. Elmer didn't worry about much but he knew this bear was one to be feared.

This morning a hard white frost covered the forest floor, and only some small areas below trees that still held some leaves had not been touched. Elmer lay under such a tree surveying the scene before him with his family. This was the first hard frost that the pups had experienced and both showed great interest in this new thing. Buster put his nose up against the cold whiteness, pushing it, sniffing it hard and then pawing it firmly but inquisitively. He straightened up and stood tall on the frozen forest floor, seemingly amazed at how the leaves, now white, had become hard and brittle, a different texture to what he had previously known.

For the next few minutes Buster took great delight in stamping around on the frozen leaves, feeling them crumble under his large paws. Meg was just as interested in this new attack on her senses but held back and watched her bolder brother as he happily tested things out. Buster was now jumping high up in the air and landing with all four feet at the same time in a sustained effort to crush as many frozen things as possible. Elmer and Freya lay together enjoying the sight of their enthralled son.

Winter was truly just around the corner now, the colder weather and shorter days had put into motion the replacement of the wolves summer coats with much thicker and warmer, winter fur.

The hunting of late had been good for Elmer and his family. Fallow deer bucks were starting their rut and the aggressive fighting to find the strongest male would sometimes result in serious injuries, leading to a telling weakness or worse. Also, the advancing years of some of the older bucks might finally catch up with them in these demanding times, making them more even more susceptible to predation.

The fallow deer doe's would traverse the forest at this time, looking for the best male suitor, and were just as driven as the bucks by the intense urge to breed, making them less wary and easier to hunt too; all good things for the wolf. The fallow deer always rutted a little earlier than their much larger cousins, the red deer. Now was their time.

Elmer's forest held many ancient stands: an area where a dominant fallow deer buck would wait and perform in the hope of attracting females. The bucks would take up their places on these century old stands, covering the immediate area and themselves in their own urine as a powerful sign to others of their kind that this was their spot. Throughout the rutting period the bucks Adams apple in their necks would stick out further than normal, a sign of increased testosterone and the readiness within them to mate, they also made loud belching noises to advertise their whereabouts and further attract the doe's. All other male adversaries that came along would be taken on in a show of strength.

The dominant bucks were so driven to attract, keep, and breed with as many females as possible that they didn't even have time to eat, throughout the rut they starved, and towards the end of it would be tired, weak and sometimes gravely injured. When two males of equal standing rutted the forest all around would fill with the noise of their clashing antlers as they fenced for the right to breed, occasionally ending in one of them paying the ultimate price. The rut gave obvious advantages to the clever and ever opportunistic wolf.

The whole family could hear the loud clashing of antlers as two mature bucks started to fight in the near distance. They were a fair way off but Elmer rose quickly to his feet, and after one long sleep destroying shake, headed straight towards them. Elmer was hoping the deer would be so engrossed in their battle that they would be able to get close to them before they were detected.

Freya and Meg were quick to follow in Elmer's path. Buster was still happily crushing frozen leaves and chewing through little twigs that had become extra snappy, eventually giving up when he realised the others were well gone, and sprinting to catch up.

Elmer knew that there would be some fallow deer doe's in the area searching from stand to stand in search of the best buck, if they came across any on the route in he would go for them as they were always an easier proposition than the larger testosterone fuelled and well armed males.

The fight between the two bucks was intense, they were well matched and the effort required was draining them both. The forceful clashing of wide spread palmate antlers grew ever louder as the wolves closed on the warring deer. Elmer gave a quick glance back to Buster and Meg; the pups slowed, letting their parents move ahead. Elmer had not come across the sign of any doe's on the route in and decided now that the two fighting bucks would be their target today.

The two fallow deer were totally focused in their own battle for supremacy and unaware of the fast approaching danger, no stealth was required as Elmer moved into position and waited for Freya to move around to the far side; she moved on the downwind side to remain undetected.

Elmer didn't want to move in too soon. He would wait and let the bucks carry on fighting for as long as possible, let them use up as much of their own strength and reserves before he charged in. Freya was in position now and she waited for Elmer to make his move. Elmer watched them closely and knew he probably wouldn't be able to take one of these large bucks straight down, they would have to inflict some damage then chase and run them down.

Buster and Meg tried their best to watch things unfold, they didn't want to get too close and give things away but both, especially Buster, felt a strong urge to join in the hunts. On some previous hunts they had tried to get involved and the result was more often failure for their parents. Their father had never chastised them for this though, as he was always happy to see their enthusiasm for the hunt. Freya was not so forgiving though, she would give them both the stare, and it was memories of those looks that now kept Buster next to his sister.

Elmer's waiting paid off. One of the bucks had weakened more than the other and was being pushed backwards violently by the stronger. In a final bid to push back the lesser buck broke one stem of his antlers completely off. The dominant buck quickly drove home his advantage, steaming forwards with all his remaining strength, goring the retreating buck on his now undefended side and pushing him over, then bull dozing him through the undergrowth.

This was what Elmer had been waiting for. He seized the moment and rushed in from behind the injured buck. The dominant buck saw him coming and turned tail to be greeted by Freya dashing in from the other side. The weaker buck was now back on his feet but seriously wounded, momentarily ignoring his pain and running on a spurt of adrenalin he turned slightly to make his escape, but Elmer was already on him: he grabbed the buck by one of his rear legs.

Freya ignored the winning buck and let him pass her as she closed quickly on Elmer to help him. Elmer had a good hold and hung on for all he was worth, evolution had given him great strength and his jaws the ability to hang on to a wild and thrashing prey animal. Freya joined him and was now attacking the rear of the deer on the opposite side. The buck, though gravely wounded, was still strong, and not yet fully aware of his own injuries. Elmer would have to let go soon or get injured himself, for this deer was heavier than him. He let go.

The buck took off with his attackers in pursuit, the chase though, was not long. Wounded heavily by the other buck and less so by Freya's quick initial attack, he was soon struggling. The deer slowed quickly, then came to a standstill.

Motionless, silhouetted in the eerie light cast from the half shade of nearly leafless young beech trees, he waited. Adrenalin now exhausted and head bowed, the shock was setting in. Elmer and Freya circled and he offered little resistance when they came in, Elmer easily pulling him down. It was all over. Together they had triumphed again over an adversary that could have, if not for their own skills and experience, caused them some damage or worse.

The pups had excitedly followed the short chase a small distance behind, and they now came tearing in to join their parents on the kill. It was a fine meal and would feed them all for a couple of days. There was no fighting at the kill, the pups were still young enough to have some special status though occasionally they squabbled between themselves.

The familiar raven was quickly on the scene, accompanied now by another smaller raven that was always with him; she was his new partner. Other scavengers were quick to follow and took up temporary residency in the trees around the kill. Freya watched them closely as she ate, her eyes conveying a look of hatred to the hungry thieves around her, most of them knew her ways and none would come down.

Later, and with bellies full, the whole family moved away from the kill to rest, Freya didn't go too far though. The temperature now was low enough to allow food buried in a cache to last a while before it spoiled but neither Elmer nor Freya felt the need to start caching yet.

It had not been long since feeding and the pups were already stirring, the good feelings from the successful hunt had not gone away and they now channelled them into some play. Elmer felt the urge too and was quick to respond to his pup's advances. Some rough wrestling followed, Elmer concentrating his attention on one pup at a time while the other attacked him from behind. Freya watched them play while still keeping one eye on their kill, occasionally she would rush over to the carcass, sending the braver scavengers squawking back up into the trees. On previous occasions, when prey was easy to come by, Freya had relented and let the birds have a feed, but not today, mother nature was telling her that much colder times were just around the corner and she would do her utmost to ensure her family were well fed.

Night time descended, clear and crisp, it would be a cold one. Elmer and his family would stay near the carcass tonight, they settled down under a beech tree. The wind was building and the recently fallen leaves were being whipped up and scattered wildly around them, some of the larger trees still had a few leaves winning the battle to hang on but they didn't offer the same protection from the weather as before; lying together under them still felt good though.

The family would not need to go off looking for food tonight. Elmer, contented and resting, passed his leisurely gaze over them. Buster met his fathers wandering eyes with his own, wide awake ones, it was as though he had been waiting for it. The youngster looked on expectantly for his father's response. Elmer got to his feet and stepped sideways over to Freya, falling into her and pushing his head into her side, a deep but gentle grumble coming from him. Buster was already on his feet now and heading over to join in, he was excited and hoping that the outward signs of obvious contentment would end in one of his favourite family activities, not play, but howling.

Meg, sensing something was afoot, got up and trotted over too, joining her brother in the mass of wriggling bodies. All four now pushed against each other, whining and whimpering as they built themselves up towards the inevitable outcome. Elmer sprung to his feet from the pile of bodies and watched closely by all his family walked slightly away from them.

The moon was not full but it was casting a strong light tonight. Elmer moved to some slightly higher ground a few yards away and stood still, body perfectly silhouetted. Sitting down on his haunches he laid back his formidable head. Freya could make out well his powerful outline, his tilted back head looking skywards, and though she couldn't see it, she imagined the closed eyes and joyous look that she knew he would have.

The still, cold, wintry silence erupted once again as Elmer drew his powerful song from the very depths of his soul. His first howl was long, deep and uninterrupted. As the warm air from his insides mingled with the cold air of the night a long thin cloud of whiteness developed, rising from his mouth up into the moonlit sky and melting away. That picture of Elmer, and the stirring sound of his howling, had the usual catching effect on the rest of the family, especially Freya. They all jumped up and found a comfortable seated position, moving their backsides about until it felt just right. The howling that followed had a passion and noise to it like never before. The pups were getting better at it.

Any forest creature within five miles that cold night could have drawn only one conclusion from what they heard; a family of wolves that was confident and bonded like no other lived here, this was their land, and like all wolves, they truly loved to howl.

CHAPTER 22

THE SNOW

The first snow of the year was falling. Elmer and Freya had seen it every year of their lives so far but it was new for Buster and Meg. Both pups were captivated by the wet white stuff that fell relentlessly from the skies.

Buster's tongue shot out as far as it would go and licked all around his face grabbing the loose white powder and sucking it in; it tasted just like cold water. The snow lay quickly on the cold dry ground and Meg pranced around in it, the different feeling and texture of it arousing her curiosity. Some young animals might have been worried about this new thing, but not Buster and Meg, they were both bold pups, especially Buster, things like this held interest for them rather than fear. Elmer had decided they would stay put today and let the pups play and get used to this new thing, he knew it would temporarily change their homeland and affect the way they travelled and hunted in it.

Meg watched her mother as she ate some of the white stuff, and copied her. Freya had watched her own mother do the same when she was a pup and now Meg was learning from her mother that snow was a source of water. Freya's thoughts about this interaction somehow made her feel good. Buster had also found out that snow could be a source of water too, but he had done it on his own by eating large mouthfuls of it as he excitedly bulldozed through it with his head down.

The snow fell heavily for most of the day. The large oak that the family were laying under was bare now and the snow built up in deep drifts on the larger branches and boughs. Sometimes, a strong gust of wind would dislodge some and it would come crashing to the ground with a dull heavy thud, making the pups jump.

The day was spent playing in the snow, then snoozing in it. When it was time for a nap, the pups copied their parents, curling up in a ring shape and burying their heads under their tails to keep the wind and snow from their faces; their oak tree may not have given such good protection overhead now but it still offered some shelter from the wind with it's large, wide trunk.

Elmer cast his searching eyes around their white homeland. The familiar raven and his new partner could be easily seen in the trees above him, their shiny black bodies standing out against the gleaming new snow. Occasionally a red squirrel entered his vision as it busily searched the snow for the acorns that it had buried in the ground months before, stopping to dig one up when it was in the right spot. Elmer watched the little red gnawer's rushing around and harboured some sort of respect for these little creatures that worked tirelessly to survive in his forest, they were active all year long. It wouldn't stop him eating one though if the need arose.

It was soon dark. Elmer wanted to patrol tonight, his young charges needed to get used to moving through the snow and it had been a couple of days since he properly marked their land. The snow had covered everything and although Elmer's sign could still be smelt through it, that familiar urge to re-lay claim to their home was surging through him.

Buster and Meg had been puzzling over how things seemed to be so much brighter and easier to see tonight, everything was white and the glare from it seemed to lighten things just a little, for sure when the moon made an appearance through the clouds the light that it shed was somehow more intense than normal.

The total whiteness would make approaching prey at night much harder to do, but Elmer also knew that the snow could give the wolf an advantage. He had learnt these things from his own parents and now he would teach them to his own family. Freya knew too the advantages that the snow could bring, she was more tactical in her hunting than most wolves and like her partner looked forward to passing that knowledge on to their offspring. Life would be easier for Elmer and herself if their family were all good hunters, but she always felt within her, that none would be as good as her.

Elmer rose to his feet and shook the remaining loose snow from his body then trotted over to a nearby tree, to leave his mark. Freya followed him and left her own mark on the tree next door, to back him up. Buster and Meg stood side by side now, nudging heavily into each other, watching and waiting eagerly for Elmer to move off. Buster was getting a little impatient and with a playful growl turned to his sister, mouthing her on the back of her head. She pushed back against him and returned a growl that was just a little less playful. Meg had her serious head on. Buster trotted off untroubled to take his place behind his now departing parents. Meg brought up the rear.

The snow was already a few inches deep but easy for the wolves to move in, the pups were enjoying the new feelings of it under their paws. A wolf's feet were large and webbed, and spread out as they walked, making the pressure exerted on the snow much less than for other similar sized creatures.

As the depth of snow increased the hunting wolf would be at a distinct advantage over much of their prey, who, with smaller and heavier loaded feet, would punch through the snow to a greater depth, making it harder and more tiring for them to move through it. Elmer would soon show the pups the advantage of this for real.

Elmer marked regularly as the family moved, sometimes Freya too. A very interested Buster would sniff the marks after his parents had moved on in the hope of finding something out, he was a little intrigued by the way his parents urine disappeared deep into the cold snow and by the visible hot air that rose from it afterwards, he had never seen such before.

Most of the familiar paths through the forest had now disappeared under the carpet of white but Elmer easily followed them with his nose, moving at a leisurely pace he made his way to the very top of their land. A much larger pack lived above them, the same pack that the large female intruder came from months before, and the ones who had ventured briefly into their land weeks ago. He would patrol the very edge of it and reinforce it with his sign. Elmer moved even more confidently in his own land, his larger and much more formidable family now behind him.

Both pups were almost adult size now, Buster was already bigger than most wolves to be found here and although still an inexperienced juvenile would be a visible deterrent to any wolves that might come looking. Elmer knew too that like himself his son would be fearless and brave where the protection of his family and their territory was concerned.

Elmer reached the top of their land and slowed to investigate it more thoroughly. This strip of land laid between the two packs territories and in the summer he had discovered the sign of others here. He found nothing to worry him and after marking in his favourite spots he moved his family on. They headed back down the edge of their land on the mountain side, patrolling along the edge of the forest. The meadows, just weeks before, had been bursting with flowers and long grasses, now they were flat and completely white. The wolf family cast their eyes over the vast white table that stretched from the forest edge to the mountains.

Buster and Meg could now see how hunting in their land when it was like this, would be much harder to do. Rabbits, that were easy to catch in warmer times now had no brush to hide in, which also meant no camouflage for the wolf. In times like this, if a wolf wanted to catch a rabbit or hare, then a flat out long distance chase was almost always the only way. If the snow got too deep for the rabbits to reach their food underneath they would have to rely on tree bark from the forest edge for nourishment, but many would perish, leaving less for the predators.

Elmer and Freya continued marking as they moved, while Buster and Meg explored whatever they came across of interest. When the pups became more used to moving in the snow they would stay in the tracks of the wolves ahead of them, to make it easier for themselves and conserve energy, but today the pups were not thinking about tactics, they just wanted to explore this new thing and the changes it brought, their antics wouldn't get too out of hand though, Freya's occasional backward glances seeing to that; they had to keep up.

The snow finally stopped falling and Elmer halted to shake of the remnants of it from his fur. It must have been catching as the whole family stopped and did the same. With the job of patrolling and marking temporarily suspended Buster thought now was a good a time as any to play and he pounced on his unwary sister, pulling her down quickly and holding her there for a second. As soon as he released her she was up and after him, a look of real anger and aggression on her face for she was not expecting it.

Buster looked back over his shoulder as she closed on him, a definite look of enjoyment on his face, even though he was about to be told off by her. He loved this, knowing he was much bigger and stronger than her, he always took her reprimands as a game, which only made her even more mad. Elmer and Freya moved beside each other, they spent some time rubbing against each other and enjoying some closeness whilst their youngsters played.

Elmer let his pups have some fun for a while but it was soon time to get back to the serious task of patrolling. The family set off again in single file. They had only covered a couple of miles when three adult, fallow deer bucks emerged from the wood ahead of them. The rut was now over for them, no longer were they arch rivals, so they moved around together in small bachelor groups. Even from this distance, and in the the low light, Elmer could tell they were all fit, strong and healthy. Buster and Meg stared with real purpose at the deer but they would not be prey tonight. The trio turned and moved slowly but meaningfully back into the woods. Elmer thought that maybe a few more weeks of heavy snow might bury the deer's food deeper, in turn leading to weaker deer as they struggled to reach it, making them easier targets. Time would tell, for now though they would let them go on their way.

Elmer set off again following the tree line along to the very bottom of their land, another pack lived beyond this point too. He would mark their boundaries here with his usual vigour before heading back into the trees to find a place to rest.

It was almost daylight by the time they finished their patrol, all the family would sleep well into the next morning.

CHAPTER 23

THE FIRST REAL HUNT IN THE SNOW

It had been a week since the first snows and in places it now lay deep enough to almost reach Elmer's elbows. Buster and Meg had quickly learnt that following their parents in strict file, with the adults breaking the trail, was much easier than making their own way. Buster was always impressed by how easily his father moved through the snow; it seemed effortless to him.

The family had taken some smaller prey over the last few days, the odd hare and rabbit that they had chased down, and a small roe deer. Elmer had his serious hunting head on this morning and all the family knew it. After the usual whines, howls and boisterous barging they set off. Buster brought up the rear, tail wagging vigorously from side to side as he followed his family through the snow, along with playing and howling, going off to hunt was one of the best feelings for him.

Both pups were now physically indistinguishable from adult wolves, their occasional youthful behaviour only giving them away to ones that would know, they still had much to learn though and Elmer, as always, relished the task of showing them.

A familiar scent crossed Elmer's track, the strength of it telling him the owner was not long in the area. He changed direction to follow it. The whole family had smelt it too and like Elmer they happily increased their speed as they got on the scent.

The red deer that inhabited the family's forest went through their rut a little later than the fallow deer, and many were still in the throes of it. Being late in the rutting season Elmer knew that most combatants would be tired and weak by now, like the fallow deer they also did not eat as they went through their rut, and often, they would get injured.

Only a few minutes had passed when he caught sight of the slow moving stag ahead of him. The loner had already caught some of their scent as Elmer had not been able to move into the wind; but he had not run off. Ambush tactics would be virtually impossible in this barren white environment, straight chase and harass tactics would be best, but first Elmer wanted to take a proper look at him.

The stag swung round to face the approaching threat, although near to the end of his rutting period and low in weight he was still easily twice as heavy as Elmer, well armed and in pretty good condition: he could not be taken lightly. The deer was a fairly young stag and as such had not rutted as much as some of the older males for he knew he would lose, the result of this was he had expended less energy in the last few weeks and so was less tired.

Elmer was unsure about this one and showed it by slowing right down and circling the beast. He wanted to be sure. The rest of the family followed his lead and circled too, with Freya occasionally darting in and out to gauge the stags reactions, strength and resolve. Buster and Meg circled but kept their distance, they wanted to help but also didn't want to get in the way. The wolf family carried on their harassing tactics, waiting for Elmer's decision.

This stag was still too strong and healthy. Elmer decided it would be too much of a risk. They couldn't risk injury at the moment, not in this weather. Elmer turned abruptly away from the young male and trotted off. The rest of the family got the message and quickly followed him on. The stag turned back onto his original path, his body still stiff and bristling from the encounter. Defiantly, he pranced off the opposite way, a final sign to the departing wolves that he was indeed one not to be messed with, and that they shouldn't change their minds. Today had been a good day for him.

Elmer looked back behind him to make sure all his family were following. They were all there and he continued on to find some easier prey. Several miles later and having found no sign of prey he decided to stop for a while, Buster immediately taking the chance for a bit of play. Unusually, Meg was quick and eager to respond and both expended some of their pent up frustration at not finding any suitable prey. Elmer and Freya rubbed against each other, licking, nuzzling and enjoying each others close company as their youngsters let off some steam. Buster and Meg had both noticed the increasing closeness and intimacy that was developing between their parents lately.

The high up, wispy clouds that had dotted the sky during the day quickly melted away, and so did any heat that might be kept in by them. The air became clear and crisp. It would be a very cold night. Elmer knew these sort of nights often brought a coldness that could freeze the top layer of snow overnight, the morning bringing a thick crust to it's surface. As heavy as Elmer was his wolf paws were made such that they were able to spread his weight allowing him, most of the time, to move over these frozen crusts without breaking through them, something that the smaller hoofed prey animals could not do, this would give the wolf a great advantage. They would settle in for the night and see what the morning brought for them.

Elmer had been right. The snow glistened and glinted as the weak early morning light reflected in all directions from it's frozen crystals, a thick crust covered the softer snow beneath. These were ideal hunting conditions and the obvious enthusiasm in Elmer's face and body was contagious. After a short burst of excited vocalisations, barging and body shakes the family was quickly and eagerly on the move, they now had to find something to hunt. Elmer headed for an area that he knew sometimes held small herds of female fallow deer. After the rut and breeding had taken place the doe's would congregate and move around in herds for protection; the senses of many were better than one.

The crust on top of the snow was holding their weight most of the time, occasionally the heavier Elmer or Buster might go through it but generally it held. Buster and Meg were well aware of this new phenomenon as they trotted happily along, but still unaware of its significance. Both though, like their parents, were eager to find some prey.

Elmer's knowledge was sound. The scent of deer started to drift towards them, but they would not be able to sneak up on them now the forest was so bare and white. Elmer headed straight for them.

The many pairs of watching eyes and acute ears had forewarned the deer of the approaching wolves, but they still waited to see their attackers. Freya went to the front as they closed, she was the fastest and if an obviously injured animal was among them she might catch it quickly, giving the others time to get to, and help her subdue it.

As soon as the deer caught site of Freya moving flat out they took off. There were no obviously injured animals in the moving herd but one had instantly caught her eye, just a little slower than the rest, she looked like she might be trying to hide something, to make herself look fitter than she was. Freya made a beeline for her.

Elmer and the pups had seen the slower deer too and were hot on Freya's tail. The doe was still moving quickly but the crust on top of the snow was having the desired effect, her small hooves were punching through with every step and sinking down deeply into the softer snow underneath, making it further for her to retrieve them from. Freya didn't sink into the snow and seemed to glide across the top of it, she was soon up behind the slowing deer. It looked like Freya was getting even faster but really the deer was getting more tired, her well hidden injury now beginning to tell.

The rest of the family were not far behind. Now and then Elmer would stumble slightly as his weight took him through the crust, he would become a little frustrated at this but quickly gathered himself and got back to full speed.

Freya was right on the deer's rear now. The tiring doe turned sharply several times to try and throw her off but Freya was ready for it and stayed right behind her. In a last ditch attempt to evade her pursuer the panicking deer tried to carry out a very sharp turn, the pressure was too much and one of her legs temporarily gave way under her, causing her to slip. It was all that Freya needed, she cut the corner off and made contact with the rear of the doe. Freya wasn't strong enough to pull it straight down but Elmer was. She held on for a second until Elmer arrived and hit it hard, knocking her straight down. Both pups were quick to join their parents and the struggle was promptly over.

The usual raven and his partner were soon at the scene of the kill, alone for now they perched silently in the snow covered limbs of a barren oak tree, surveying the scene below. To the watching ravens the family now looked like four adults together, and they had appetites to match. The dead doe was not one of the largest, it's injury maybe limiting growth, but it was still a good meal for them. They would consume nearly all of it in one sitting.

Elmer was pleased with how the hunt had gone, it was the first in the snow for Buster and Meg and although they did not yet add any real help it would have been a good lesson for them. Both Buster and Meg had learnt today that when hunting fallow deer doe's in snow a fast approach was usually best, that quickly weeding out your target was paramount with these fleet footed deer, and most important of all, that a thick crust on top of the snow gave the wolf a definite advantage over their fleeing prey; lessons that they would both remember.

Thirty minutes later little remained of the carcass. The whole family retired a short distance away from the blood stained, fur covered snow, to rest and enjoy the feeling of being full. Elmer and Freya rolled in the snow to help clean their faces and fur before settling. Buster and Meg copied their parents.

Several hours later the contented dozing of the wolf family was interrupted by the ever present and vigilant ravens; they were tuning up loudly. Deep, raucous warning calls croaked their way out from the treetops and through the air, reaching deep into the wolves ears. Elmer reacted first, springing to his feet and searching immediately for any possible threat that the ravens might have seen. The others were soon on their feet too, standing tall and scanning hard the surrounding area. It was Buster who was the first to see the danger, a long deep growl rolled out of his mouth.

The ground around them was fairly flat but there were parts about that stood slightly higher. Buster growled deeper and longer at the distant creature, it stood silhouetted on top of one of those higher bits of land and wanted to be seen. The intruder was another wolf, it was well inside their territory. As they watched another wolf appeared beside it, then another, then another.

Elmer stared long and hard at the trespassers, then, without any sound, he headed off directly towards them. Freya and the pups were instantly behind him, the whole family accelerated into a fast trot towards the enemy.

CHAPTER 24

FAMILY IS EVERYTHING

The intruders did not leave their higher position. Elmer kept his eyes fixed on them while moving. He would lead his family up the incline to the side and approach from there, so they were on the same level as them when they met: he didn't want to be at the disadvantage of attacking straight uphill.

The slight hill and deep snow seemed like nothing to Elmer and his family. Adrenalin, the fuel of war, was building up within them the closer they got. There was only a few hundred yards between them now and Elmer moved even faster, all the time keeping his eyes fixed on the intruders, letting them know that he meant business.

They were still there. Buster moved past Freya now and came up onto his fathers shoulder. Elmer briefly stole a look across to him and felt himself grow even taller as he witnessed the intense look of fearlessness, and willingness to do battle, in his young son. They were a formidable force.

The other wolves were now becoming restless. Unknown to Elmer there were six of them, two more were behind in the lower ground, but none came close to the size of him or his son. The leader of the intruders was the breeding male from the neighbouring pack and he was now having second thoughts about the outcome as these two huge wolves and their pack closed on him.

That morning, when the leader of the neighbouring pack had left to invade Elmer's land, his partner had known what was on his mind, but she hadn't joined him. She was the large female that entered Elmer's land months before with two of her yearlings. Elmer had let her leave then without causing any major harm and she had not forgotten him. This morning she had stayed in her homeland with this years pups, and the two from last year.

Elmer's family moved as one, all their outward signals giving of a message of strength and unity as they powered, without worry, towards their foe. The leader of the trespassers was now unsure if he had done the right thing this morning. He looked quickly behind him to his own pack members and could see tiny signs of fear and trepidation looking back at him. Better to leave and fight another day he thought. Turning quickly he moved his pack back the way they had come, the obvious signs of relief and a willingness to follow him were plain.

Seconds later Elmer reached the spot where the intruders had stood, and went no further. Buster wanted to carry on the chase and see them off completely, but his father was happy to watch them disappearing into the distance, back to their own land. The whole family started to whoop and whine and then howl at the success of this day. They had seen off a larger pack from their land without even having to fight, just the sight of Elmer and Buster, side by side, with Freya and Meg behind, had been enough. Today was indeed a great day.

Freya had always harboured great respect for Elmer, it had been there from the very first day they met, she greatly admired his ways and after today her feelings for him went even deeper. She had also witnessed the true character of Buster and Meg with Buster running fearlessly beside his father, at the front, ready to take on anything before him, and Meg running determinedly by her own side. They did indeed have a brave, loyal and strong family.

Meg had always known within her that her brother would be the bravest of souls, and she had seen it today. Buster himself thought little about his actions, he was doing what came naturally to one like him; backing up his father, helping him to protect his family and their land. The small wolf family renewed their bonds with mutual shows of affection and choruses of howling that carried on for over an hour, sending a strong message of unity and ownership to any that might be listening.

The happy howling now over Elmer led his family back to the site of their last kill, there would not be much of it left but they would go there anyway. As they travelled Freya thought about today's events, and she kept returning to the time when they were first warned of the possible danger from the invading wolf pack. It was the familiar raven and his partner that had alerted them from their treetop positions. The ravens actions somehow seemed to put them in a new light for her, and for once she found herself maybe understanding why Elmer was almost always tolerant of them.

As they approached the remains of the carcass the familiar raven and his partner were on it, enjoying the meagre leftovers. The big birds looked towards the approaching wolves and prepared themselves to leave and lift up into the trees. Elmer waited for Freya to rush in and claim what was left back from the birds but she didn't. She walked slowly over towards the carcass as the ravens hopped backwards, away from her. Freya cast her eyes over the red snow, just some skin and bone lay scattered about. She turned around and trotted back to lay beside her already resting partner and pups. The clever ravens, always quick to seize an opportunity, hopped back in and carried on eating the remains unmolested.

Elmer, the pups, and the familiar raven too, all noticed this difference in Freya's behaviour and wondered why. The family settled down to relax once again.

Only an hour had passed when Buster lifted his head from under the warmth of his covering tail and looked around at his family. All the others were curled up on the snow in their own circular positions, heads under their tails. Buster, still buzzing from the earlier action, was looking for a playmate, but none were forthcoming.

The pair of ravens watched from their tree as the young wolf trotted off happily through the snow. Years of association with wolves were telling the bold birds that this wolf had mischief on his mind. The male raven flew down from his perch and landed just a few yards in front of him. Buster, like his father, had never had any real problem with the ravens and he stared at it with a playful look that the raven somehow seemed to recognize. Buster rushed at the large black bird and for the first time really took stock of the actual size of them; they were one of the largest of the perching birds.

The raven bobbed up into the air, easily evading the wolf and landing again a few feet away. Buster rushed him again. Things quickly turned into a back and forth game of chase and evade; both were enjoying it. Buster was intrigued and a little thrilled by how much he was enjoying this play with the big bird, and was taken by surprise when its partner crowed a warning from the trees. His playmate quickly left, and flew back up to her. Buster looked around quickly, searching for the cause of it.

Earlier, when the young wolf had left his family in search of some fun, all were not really asleep. Meg had secretly watched him leave and after a few minutes had got up to find him. She had followed his tracks and found him already playing with the raven, and for a while had remained at a distance, watching them. Her curiosity, and maybe thoughts of interrupting her big brothers fun eventually got the better of her and she had moved forward to have a closer look. The raven's mate had seen Meg approaching and unsure of her intentions had crowed a warning to her partner on the ground. He reacted as any raven would and Buster's playfellow took to the trees.

Buster turned to see Meg approaching and was more than a little upset that his fun had been cut short by his sister, she would have to be his playmate now. He charged straight at her. Meg could easily have got out of his way and lead him on a merry chase but she didn't. She accepted her brothers head on approach with a friendly growling response, and he ploughed into her. They wrestled briefly then shot off, chasing around in the deep snow, just like they used to when much smaller pups, only months before.

Elmer and Freya were now resting alone as their youngsters played not far away. Elmer had heard the ravens call but quickly put it down to his boisterous pups, for he could now hear them playing.

Over the last few days Freya had felt the changes taking place within her, she had experienced it before, and knew what it meant; the time to breed was approaching again. Recently, Elmer had gone out of his way to lay a little closer to his mate whenever they settled, for he too knew the signs .

Freya stood up and edged even closer to Elmer, then flopped into his side. A show of mutual affection, nudges and licks followed as they further cemented their bonds, revelling in the good feelings that came with being a successful breeding pair.

The closeness between Elmer and Freya heightened over the next few days. The pups might have been adult in size but they were still juvenile in many of their ways. Often their youthful exhilaration would take over, turning their excited feelings for their parents preparations to breed into full on, overly boisterous play.

Freya was continually approaching Elmer, presenting her rear his way, letting him sniff her. With the time not far away they walked off together, leaving the pups alone. Elmer stayed close to his partner now, continually scenting her and the air, showing great interest when she urinated in the snow, smelling and tasting it. Hormones and her behaviour would all help him to gauge when she truly came into heat.

All the signs were right now, both Elmer and Freya were ready. Freya stood still before Elmer and averted her tail to one side allowing him to mount her. They would mate several times over the next few days and each time end up coupled together, sometimes for up to thirty minutes; natures way of hopefully ensuring successful copulation. Elmer also found that the whole ritual behaviour of breeding seemed to somehow reinforce his already strong bond with Freya even further. She felt the same.

This was the way breeding always took place between wolves but Elmer couldn't help but feel a little vulnerable when they were coupled together, it would be almost impossible for him to defend Freya and himself when in this position. If he really needed to the tie between them could be broken, but he still felt uneasy. Elmer didn't worry quite so much this year though, for he knew Buster and Meg would never be far away.

CHAPTER 25

TRIALS OF LIFE

The sun shone brightly this early spring morning and the crisp clean air allowed eyes to see far and wide. Elmer caste his pleasured gaze over their land and could see the areas of brown and green bursting back through the white carpet that had covered it for the last 8 weeks. The snow this year had been heavy but short and it now melted quickly as the temperature slowly rose.

Elmer and his family had done well throughout the time of the snow and the youngsters had learnt many new skills. Buster and Meg had taken these lessons seriously as they both wanted to be as successful as their parents. Hunting had gone well through the cold months and they had the opportunity to cache some food for later. The ground had been hard when they had buried it and so much of it was hidden in shallow holes, which put it at risk of discovery from other hungry critters with a nose good enough to sniff it out. Sometimes the disappearing snow would work in the wolfs favour too as it threw up a half frozen creature that had not made it through the coldest spell.

Now 11 months old the pups were as inquisitive and bold as ever, they investigated their reappearing land with obvious enthusiasm. Meg was off on her own following her nose, something of great interest was drawing her further away from her family. The scent became stronger as she trotted along head down, unworried and unaware of the distance quickly being put between her and the others. The smell that impelled her was one of food. As she moved the excitement built up within her, the anticipation of finding the next meal for her family was getting her excited. She should have got the attention of another before setting off alone.

Ahead of Meg the thawing snow had revealed an old fallow deer buck that had succumbed to the cold only weeks before. The depth of snow had made it difficult for him to reach the food below, his old age, condition, and the lack of food had been too much for his ageing body and he lay there now, waiting to be found, a veritable feast for any hungry passer by.

Meg knew she was close to the carcass and went into a stealthier mode as she approached it, the breeze blowing steadily into her face. She took several minutes to cover the last few hundred yards, there could be other hungry animals about and this carcass would be a good find. Meg finally reached her goal and stood above the body scanning the area around her. The deer lay in a small depression, remnants of snow hanging on in the bottom of it, the body was still half frozen. She reached down and pawed it with obvious interest. Meg pondered whether to try and drag it out, maybe have a feed, or go and get the rest of her family.

Her cautious approach was well founded. Another hunter had also picked up the scent of the carcass and he was stealthily following the wolf's tracks towards it. He knew that following her would not carry his scent as the wind came from his front. Meg was still on the carcass checking out the area and deciding what to do next as the large male lynx, still in his thick grey brown winter coat, approached. He could see her now but she was still unaware of the danger. The cat went into stalk mode; the feline hunter would get as close as possible before charging her. Even from this distance his nose and experience told him the wolf was female, young and alone. He should be able to scare her off with a surprise attack.

The big lynx was usually a night time hunter and would not normally have chosen to tangle with a wolf but his solitary success in hunting of late had not been as good as Meg's families. Not quite as heavy as Meg, the large cat was an explosive, powerful, ambush predator, stronger and much more experienced than the young wolf, he regularly took down full grown roe deer that were much heavier than him. As he drew closer he made up his mind that he would fight this young wolf if he had too. Meg didn't know it yet, but trouble was certainly coming her way.

Meg was still scanning the surrounding area, her back towards the unseen enemy. The Lynx made up his mind to go now and sprinted towards her, fast and quiet, his large, heavily furred feet, almost silencing his movement. He had nearly reached Meg before she sensed him, turning fast and moving quickly she just managed to deny him any sort of a grip on her. Meg was a fast wolf and instantly employed her speed to its fullest. A battle of flashing teeth and claws erupted as each tried to gain a quick advantage. She did not run.

The young wolf managed to avoid all the lynx's attempts to get a good hold on her but she was taking a lot of lesser damage. The powerful cat tried to get on her back and she rolled quickly throwing him off. Instantly he was back. The cats racking claws were much sharper and more dangerous than hers, large clumps of her fur flew into the air as they wrestled, the lynx flailing his paws wildly.

Meg should have tried to make off now but she didn't, and it quickly dawned on her that she might have made a big mistake. She could not allow him to get a grip on her neck or she too, might end up lying next to the dead deer. Meg manoeuvred her gnashing jaws about in a bid to latch on and do some damage of her own, she too had some impressive weaponry and the genes inherited from her parents were not going to let her give up easily.

The lynx dug deep and called on all of his vast experience to help him deal with this tenacious young wolf. He had hoped that a short battle would have ended in her making off but he knew now he would have to kill or seriously injure her. They were both now in a fight for their lives.

Meg had been holding her own. Her stamina was good but the lynx's greater real life experience in hunting and killing was now starting to show. The fight was loud, long and vicious and as Meg took a deep scything bite to her shoulder she cried out loudly. The big cat grew extra strength from her cries and it spurred him on. Sensing the turn in his favour he called on the very last reserves of his energy to help him win.

She would never give up, Meg too was summoning up the very last of her life force, calling on all she had learnt in her short life to help her survive; the hunts, the chases, the fights with her brother. If she was not to live then she would do as much damage as possible.

The pair battled on. The lynx becoming aggressively louder while Meg cried more often and became weaker. Only a minute had passed, it seemed like longer. Meg was losing but she would still not run. The lynx managed to get Meg on her back and sensing the end might be near struggled violently to roll her slightly, raising his head so he could seize her by the back of the neck.

146

The lynx didn't get that chance. Something smashed hard into his side and lifted him completely up and away from the young wolf below him, the force of the impact driving all the remaining air from him as his lungs collapsed. A huge black wolf, silent and immensely strong, took him sideways through the air.

As the lynx flew through the air his thoughts momentarily flashed back to the sight of the huge black wolf he had seen leading his family weeks before and how he had told himself at that time he would never want to tangle with him. The lynx's hunger had driven him to make a mistake that would now cost him his life.

The exhausted lynx, gasping for breath and disorientated, had little reserves to call on as he landed heavily on his back. Scrambling frantically, he tried to get to his feet. Elmer grabbed him savagely by the neck, and avoiding his flailing claws dragged him quickly across the ground, ragging him violently as he went. Elmer wouldn't allow him to get to his feet and gain some purchase, he might still be capable of doing some damage.

Buster quickly followed by Freya now joined the fight, Buster clamping down onto the lynx's rear where his weight and strength would be employed to help hold him down, while Freya moved around attacking the rest of him. Elmer kept his vice like grip on the large cat's throat allowing him some control over its head and jaws, the most dangerous bits. The fate of the large feline predator was sealed.

Elmer made sure the big cat was truly dead before letting go his grip. The fight over Buster went straight over to his still lying and injured sister. He nuzzled and licked her and reassured her with gentle prods, willing her to get up. Meg rose slowly to her feet, she was bleeding heavily from many wounds and some were deep, she had been lucky though, her speed and tenacity had allowed her to survive just long enough until Elmer's arrival.

Less than an hour earlier Elmer had noticed the absence of Meg. She had been away a while and he easily discovered her tracks leading away from the family. Something told him he should follow them and on his own he had set off after her. Freya and Buster had both seen Elmer leave and after a minute or two of their own deliberations they had decided to follow on after him.

147

Elmer had not travelled far when he first caught the scent of the Lynx that was following closely behind his daughter. His memories jumped back quickly to the unseen lynx's kill they had taken a few months back, he knew it was the same male. Elmer lowered his head to the ground and moved instantly into a fast run.

The scent of Meg and the cat quickly grew stronger as he closed. He was only a few hundred yards away and could hear the sounds of the fierce battle ahead of him. The first of Meg's loud cries pierced his ears, giving him a speed and power he had never known before, he would not lose another daughter.

Freya and Buster were not far behind, their own senses telling them the exact same story as Elmer's, they followed on hard in his tracks. Buster too, heard Meg's loud cries ahead, and seemingly found even more speed as he left his mother behind and powered forwards.

Completely taken over by his battle with the young wolf the usually ever so vigilant lynx was blinkered to all around him, until Elmer smashed into his side. In an instant the feline killer had gone from a position of victory to one that would cost him his life.

CHAPTER 26

BROTHERLY LOVE

It had been a couple of days since the fight with the big lynx. Elmer had kept his family in the area of the deer carcass that Meg had found, he wanted to give her some time to heal. Buster had not left his sisters side, he could often be seen tenderly licking her wounds or gently nudging her to encourage some movement and interaction. Meg secretly grew great strength from her big brothers close and loving attention.

Elmer gave the signals that preceded them going off to patrol. Buster didn't join in with the usual furore so enthusiastically for he was going to stay and watch over his weakened sister, she was not yet up to serious travel. Elmer and Freya moved off.

Lately, Freya had been taking greater interest in their land as they moved through it. She was looking for suitable den sites and did not want to make the same mistakes as last time. Elmer instinctively knew what was on Freya's mind and while on their travels would willingly postpone patrolling to let her investigate an area that drew her interest. A month from now new members would be added to their family and both knew that these new pups would become the focus of all their attention.

As they travelled Elmer found his concentration being interrupted by thoughts for his family. He knew that as his pack got bigger things would change, but was sure in the knowledge that Buster and Meg would remain loyal guardians and members until their own time to leave. He was also certain that until those times did come along, Buster would make a number two that could never be bettered; this made him feel good.

Freya stopped at the foot of a slight bank. Elmer sensed she wasn't following and turned to see her disappearing into the trees. She had found the remains of an old badger's sett and wanted to have a closer look. Elmer gave a knowing look and laid himself down to one side of the track while she investigated. Freya walked slowly around the old sett, sniffing and nudging things, she thought there might be see some good potential in this site. It was on higher ground, dug into the bank of a slight hillside with the river below it and only a few minutes trot away. There was a good covering of trees on the hillside and around the sett, making it hard to see from a distance, the ground itself was firm and although some of the entrances had collapsed with the passage of time, it would still make a good den site.

She had made up her mind. This would be her primary den site. There would be a lot of work to do, expanding the main tunnel and sleeping area, as well as filling in some of the other entrances that the badgers had made, but she had a good feeling about it. For a few seconds she thought about last years mistakes, and told herself she would find a second densite before starting any work on this one.

Freya emerged from the trees and padded over to Elmer, nudging into the side of his huge head. Elmer knew from her behaviour that she had made a decision about this spot. He got up and pushed his head back into hers then trotted into the trees to have a look for himself. Elmer could see why she had picked this spot, he too had learnt from their mistakes of last year and could see good things in this place; it was Freya's decision really but he was happy with the site. He proceeded to mark and scrape the area all around vigorously, to lay some claim to it, and also to let Freya know he agreed with her choice. Freya came back in and did some marking of her own, just to seal the decision.

Deliberations and marking over, it was time to get back to the serious work of patrolling and marking their land. Elmer took the lead, his tail swishing gently from side to side as he went, happy that they had found the next den site for his expanding family, and taking the good feelings along with him. To any knowing eyes that might have spied them today they painted a picture of a breeding pair of wolves that were strong, close and totally at ease with the environment in which they moved.

Elmer and Freya trotted confidently through their land, soaking up the signs of the emerging springtime forest all around them. Some of the early spring flowers were already in full show, the small lightly coloured flowers of Snowdrops and Primroses could be seen dotted heavily among the new, bright green shoots of emerging young Bluebells, all drawing on the food and energy that was stored in their underground bulbs and root systems. In the coming weeks the Bluebells would be flowering and large areas of the forest floor would be awash with their vibrant colour and strong smelling blooms. Elmer would remember those smells well, associating them to the happy times of last year, and their first ever pups.

Back at the temporary site Buster was laying next to Meg, watching as she dozed contentedly under his ever vigilant eyes. He watched a nearby red squirrel as it busied itself taking pieces of fungi up into the trees to wedge in crevices for the sun to dry out, so he could eat it later. All seemed quiet and calm until a new noise started reaching his ears. Buster sprung upright, his erratic, noisy movement, rousing Meg from her shallow sleep. Something was approaching. Buster now stood to attention, directing his formidable head and it's senses that way. Ignoring any pain Meg followed suit to stand tall beside him. Buster moved slowly towards the stifled grunting sounds, the unseen animal was moving closer.

Buster prepared himself and moved forwards to the small crest that would allow him to see what it was that moved about below them. The noises might have been new to him but they were not loud, like a bears, and he told himself that whatever it was must be small. Reaching the high point he made himself as big as possible and looked down. A creature he had never seen before, something unknown to him, was moving around.

Not much bigger than a small rabbit and covered in spines, the creature grunted and snorted as it shuffled along, head down, pushing a long, thin nose, through the leaf litter ahead of it.

Buster barked down at it and without even looking his way the small mammal immediately curled itself up into a tight little ball. With no legs now protruding it rolled uncontrolled down the slight incline, coming to rest on the flatter, lower ground. It stayed there, still curled up, and unmoving.

The big pup rushed down the slope, leaves and twigs flying everywhere, and preceded to bounce around, growling loudly at this little thing before him. Meg watched on from the higher ground as her brother obviously puzzled over it. He gave it a clout with one of his huge paws and a little squeal came from it as it rolled away. Meg, intrigued by the noises, made her way slowly down and stood behind Buster, watching as he rolled the strange, spiky creature about.

He was getting a little frustrated now because the creature wasn't doing anything, they couldn't even chase it, he began scraping the ground up vigorously all around it with his front paws, clouting it now and then. The feel of its sharp, prickly body told Buster that this was probably not a prey item, but maybe they could play with it, if he could get it to move. For the next few minutes he rolled the creature around, often barking and growling at it. Meg was becoming uninterested now, it was too small to be any sort of threat and probably no good to eat, so she wandered back up to where she had lain.

Buster played with it for a little more but soon lost interest too, giving up to follow his sister back up. He stopped on the crest of the incline and laid down, picking a position that allowed him to watch his sister and the strange animal at the same time. Laying his head down on his big outstretched front paws, he continually shifted his deep blue eyes from Meg, to the animal, and back again.

A few minutes later some movement and rustling leaves focused Buster's attention again. The spiny creature was slowly unfurling itself. It got back to its feet, giving itself a little shake, just like a wolf did, then shuffled off at a pace that was still slow, but a little quicker than before. For a second Buster thought to run back down there and give chase, but didn't, he would stay with his sister. The hedgehog, not long from his winter hibernation, ambled off, seemingly none the worse for it's unexpected encounter.

Elmer marked their land regularly as they moved and Freya almost always backed it up with one of her own, it seemed that in the months around her time of pregnancy she was even more driven to do this, to reinforce claims on the land and strengthen their own bonds. Elmer decided to stop for a while and settled below a large, still naked oak tree. He turned his head, looking long and hard into Freya's eyes. She trotted over to him and fell into his side. Elmer lifted his head and put it on top of her neck, gently but firmly holding her down and soaking up the smell of her. Freya enjoyed the attention of her partner and visibly relaxed within his grip; both were the happiest they had ever been.

The wolf couple enjoyed the close company of each other for a time before Elmer rose to his feet. A quick, hard shake got him ready, and he set off back towards the others. On the way back Freya pushed in front of Elmer and detoured through the new den site she had found. Elmer followed her in and they had another quick look around, leaving some more sign, before Freya left and led them back to the pups.

Buster rushed out to meet his parents followed a bit more slowly by Meg. Elmer could see that his daughter was still suffering the effects of the fight and decided then that they would try and spend a few more days resting. The deer carcass was all but gone now and only scraps for the ravens remained. The family had not eaten the dead Lynx; the ravens and other scavengers had seen to that.

Elmer thought they should look for a place a little distance away to lie up, the remaining scent might well attract others and with Meg being so weak it would not be the best time to engage the family in fighting. They moved to a spot about a mile from the carcass site and settled down for a prolonged rest. Elmer lay close to Freya and Buster tightly up against his sister.

The next morning brought clear blue skies, bright sunlight and a strong cooling breeze. The wind didn't just bring cold though, it brought something else, a scent that Elmer recognized instantly. The Bear was back.

CHAPTER 27

LIFE IS NEVER EASY

The scent of the bear soaked into the nostrils of all the family. He was probably still a half mile away, but moving upwind they could smell him easily. Elmer had already made up his mind he would go and find him alone.

This bear would be too powerful in a direct confrontation, Elmer couldn't win, instead he hoped to find the bear and while remaining unseen follow him to try and work out his intentions. Freya and the others sensed he had decided to go alone and all, especially Buster, were not happy about it.

He knew that if he took his family a fight might well be the outcome and he didn't want this, Meg was not strong enough and he didn't want to give this bear any reason to stay any longer in their territory. In a few weeks their next pups would be born and it would be too dangerous to have a bear like this one in their land. If he was not to leave of his own choosing then together they might have to try and make him leave. Elmer hoped not.

Elmer trotted over to Freya and reassured her with some firm head rubbing and comforting whines before setting off. Buster followed him for the first few hundred yards, not stopping until Elmer turned and willed him to go back with his stare. Buster stood tall, his soulful blue eyes watching his father closely until he disappeared out of view, he let out a small whine, then turned and made his way back to Freya and Meg. He would do his utmost to protect them while Elmer was gone.

As he travelled, Elmer thought about the bear and remembered the look of hatred that had filled his eyes, he recalled too how unnaturally driven the bear had been in following him. Elmer found himself heading for the remnants of the deer carcass they had left the day before and felt glad that he had moved his family away from it, no doubt the bears impressive nose had smelt something of the remains. Elmer would have to move quietly and stealthily, there was still little foliage to hide him, parts of the forest floor were deep in decomposing leaves and twigs that helped with camouflage but they were noisy to move through. Elmer was glad though, that the snow had long gone, he would have been easy to spot in it.

Elmer took to a small ridge that was downwind from the remains and ran parallel and above the route that he thought the bear would be taking. He hoped to be able to see him without being detected and follow from a distance, not wanting to give this dangerous predator any reason to stay and pursue him. Elmer knew the bear would easily smell the scent of his family around the kill area, but hopefully if he was not to actually see them, he might give up and go on his way.

The big brown bear had spent the winter in a den outside of Elmer's land and had only recently emerged. Hibernation had reduced the bears weight by nearly half and with the driving force of intense hunger behind him he immediately went on the search for food. The bears fantastic sense of smell had been successful in leading him to some small scraps of carrion remains but he still had a desire within him that was all consuming. He was on a mission.

Elmer spied him. Several hundred yards away the bear was moving slowly towards the site of the old deer carcass. Elmer was sure there would be nothing left by now, the assorted scavengers would have cleaned everything up. He watched as the thinner but still huge bear let out a long deep roar and charged into the carcass area; no doubt a reaction to the scent all around of Elmer and his family.

The bear ambled around the site, letting out low rumbling grunts and sniffing hard, he was agitated that nothing was left for him and his behaviour grew wilder and louder. The giant bear moved slowly around the whole area in a feverish search for any missed scraps, meat that might have been buried by others; but there was nothing to be found. Elmer sat still on his haunches, just a few hundred yards downwind, looking silently on.

An hour later and unsuccessful in his search for any thing of worth the bear moved off. Elmer stalked the bear from a distance for the next few hours, eventually following him to the meadows that fringed their forest. The bear must have been truly hungry. Elmer watched him several times try half heartedly to rip open a rabbit warren with his ten centimetre claws, then becoming highly aggravated by his fruitless efforts; he had precious little energy to waste.

Still moving into the wind and undetected, Elmer moved along the edge of the forest, shadowing the ambling bear. They made their way to the top of the territory, all the time the large disgruntled carnivore sniffing the air heavily, while staying in the open ground of the meadows, making for much easier travelling for him.

Elmer was moving slowly with stealth and focus, but then, for just a second or two, found his attention drawn away from his task. A large dark shape moved slowly across the ground in front of him. He looked up to see a golden eagle, soaring majestically and soundlessly overhead. The female eagles were much bigger than their male counterparts, and with a wingspan wider than Elmer was long, she floated effortlessly on the breeze. The eagle posed no threat to him but they could take full grown foxes and easily take a young, unprotected wolf pup. He made a mental note of its appearance in his land and stored it away; they would be having new pups again soon.

The bear was approaching the edge of Elmer's land. He would be heading into the neighbouring packs territory soon and Elmer was happy that they would now have to deal with him. Relieved that this true menace was leaving their land he felt like advertising the fact with some celebratory howling, but he curbed the urge; he didn't want to risk doing anything to bring him back this way.

Elmer knew only too well that bears lived a long time and felt sure their paths might one day cross again. He turned and headed back to his family.

Buster stood statue like, strong and alert at the sign of approach. The tenseness within him visibly drained away as Elmer came into view and he rushed forward to greet his father. Freya was close behind him while Meg, just as enthusiastically but more slowly, brought up the rear. A few minutes of mutual bonding and excitable behaviour ensued as the family made good their bonds. Elmer had not been gone long but all the family were happy to see him back.

Elmer thought about the rest of the day and decided they would spend it laying together, soaking up the family feelings until dusk when he would take Freya off to do some hunting. Buster would stay and watch over Meg.

It was dusk now. Buster lay close to Meg as Elmer set off with Freya following closely behind. Elmer moved quicker than normal, heading back to the meadows that he had travelled in earlier that day. He had his hunting head on but also had something more on his mind, he wanted to reassure himself that the bear had truly left their land. Freya could easily smell the lingering sign of the giant as they moved and knew well the purpose of the route that Elmer took.

Elmer kept to the woods like he had earlier and travelled up to the spot where the bear had left their territory. They investigated the area thoroughly, both wanting to be sure in their own minds that the danger had gone. No recent sign of the bear could be found and a noticeably happier Elmer turned back from the edge of his land and headed eagerly for the meadows.

The night was an inky black one, little light being cast by the new moon. Daily temperatures were slowly rising but the nights were still cold; it didn't bother the wolf though. Seeing in the darkness was not a problem for them either, evolution had given Elmer and Freya a pair of eyes that were better than most at night, especially their preys.

Elmer could make out a small deer browsing on the edge of the tree line ahead of them. It was a Roe deer buck, grazing on root shoots and any shrubs that were about. The smallest of the deer to be found in their forest they generally moved about alone. The buck was about seventy pounds in weight; not the heaviest but still a good meal. Roe deer rutted much earlier than the other deer and the velvet that now covered his small antlers would soon be rubbed off, ready for their rut in a few months time.

Freya had seen him too now and slowly she moved out into the meadow, if he made a run for it into the more open ground she would have the best chance of catching him. The buck was unaware of the approaching wolves and carried on feeding, he was good at seeing movement during the day but at night his sight was limited; smell and hearing were his night time senses.

Elmer moved along the edge of the tree line hugging it tightly so as not to silhouette himself, he wouldn't venture into the forest yet, moving through the heavy forest floor debris would no doubt give him away.

Luck often played a role in a wolfs hunting success and Elmer was tonight hoping the Buck would take to the open meadow and his fleet footed partner in a bid to escape him. The roe deer was not the fastest of their kind, but they were still capable of good speed, the dark night though, would give the wolf an advantage in this chase.

Elmer knew all his quarry well, Roe deer would nearly always bark when they first became frightened or anxious; he would take this as his sign to rush in. He was now only twenty yards from the buck, so close he could hear him chewing on some fodder. Elmer used the continuous sound of the feeding buck as a sign of it's unknowing and moved closer.

The chewing stopped and so did Elmer. He prepared himself as the nervous bucks first barks filled the air. Without waiting for any more he rushed in. In a bid to get the buck to take to the meadow Elmer moved further into the wood as he closed. He need not have worried, the buck took straight to the meadow and the easier route of escape for one with good speed and lesser eyes.

Elmer burst back into the meadow and gave chase but he was not really gaining. Still not quite sure exactly where Freya was he kept the pressure on. There she was. A flash of lighter colour came dashing in from the right. Freya was right on the deer's rear as it dodged and tried to escape her. Freya was fast but it was not her speed that would be the telling factor tonight.

A combination of low light, lesser vision and growing panic within the fleeing deer caused him to run flat out into a large, solid clump of grass, the result saw him cart wheeling through the air.

Freya was on him as soon as he hit the ground. The bucks hoofs kicked wildly and he thrashed his head about in an attempt to do some damage with his small, two pronged antlers, to give him a chance of escape. Freya could only just hold the struggling deer down, if she moved to try and get a better grip it might get away. She was relieved when Elmer finally joined her. The buck's most dangerous weapons were his small, pointed antlers, Elmer grabbed him by the neck to control them. The struggle was quickly over.

The buck was too heavy to carry back to the others in one piece, had Meg been well they would all have been here. Elmer and Freya would eat their fill now and what was left would be carried back to the pups. Unlike most other wolves there was no aggression on the kill as they ate, Elmer would even hold the carcass still while Freya pulled a chunk off for herself. As long as prey was plentiful and they were successful in catching enough Elmer saw no reason to be dominant around it. Soon though, there would be even more mouths to feed and the larger the pack the more order would have to be maintained.

Buster and Meg were already on their feet peering into the darkness expectantly. They knew their parents were coming. Both could now make out the carcass that Elmer was carrying and they sprinted out to greet them. Meg, caught up in the furore, almost managed to keep up with her brother, a testament to her youthful health and recuperative capabilities. She still had a way to go but both Elmer and Freya could see her improvement.

The fresh meat went down well. Freya watched Buster as he used his considerable strength to hold the carcass still, making it easier for his weakened sister to pull large chunks off. A good feeling came over Freya as she likened the behaviour to that of her partners, when earlier that night he had held the same carcass still for her. Buster was indeed, just like his father.

CHAPTER 28

THE OTTER

All the family, even Meg, were keen to get moving around their territory again but Elmer decided to stay here until the next day before taking the family off again, it would give Meg a little more time.

Freya was feeling the need to seek out a second den site and start work on them both. Elmer could see plainly the urges within her and knew he would soon have to start turning his attention more to the needs of Freya and their forthcoming pups.

The following morning brought strong spring sunshine accompanied by the usual dawn chorus of the many feathered creatures about. Elmer lay still and listened. Many of the birds were singing louder and longer than normal, it was also their time of year to start a new family, to try and attract a mate, and like the wolf, they also sang beautifully to advertise their presence and claim their little bit of the forest.

Elmer wanted to watch for a while. He had become intrigued, observing one particular little bird before him as it toiled away tirelessly to close the opening of an old woodpecker's hole with wet mud. Eventually the entrance hole on the side of the big oak tree was reduced to a size that would only allow a bird so small to squeeze through. Later the mud would dry to a colour similar to the bark, making it hard for any to make out; a safer place then for the next generation of nuthatches to be born within.

With the work of the tiny bird nearly done Elmer found his eyes drawn away by the movement of a female blackbird as it landed on the branch of a nearby silver birch tree, she looked quickly around then descended into the leaf litter below. Elmer watched as she threw leaf after leaf high into the air and scraped at the ground underneath with her feet, looking for the worms and other small creatures that might dwell there. Several minutes later her beak was overflowing with a multicoloured array of small worms, grubs and caterpillars. She took a furtive look around then flew back up to the same branch she came from. The mother birds head darted about constantly, surveying the scene around for any possible threats like magpies and crows, for they might well note her final destination, and later raid her nest. She hopped from branch to branch, all the time keeping a watch out, before finally diving into the thick bush that held her waiting brood within. Elmer took it all in.

Many of the forests trees were still bare and the strong sunlight made it's way easily onto the resting family. All the pack members did their best to soak some of it up, occasionally rolling over to get the welcome warmth on both sides of their bodies, their tails wagging slowly from side to side as they enjoyed the moment.

Freya was the first to rise to her feet, driven by the powerful urge within her to find a second densite for the coming pups. She wanted to get moving. Elmer climbed up next and like Freya stretched his sleepy body outwards. Buster and Meg watched closely, they could already tell they would be on the move today, and quickly joined their parents on all fours. The air turned loud with the usual howls, whines and the increasing bedlam of excitable behaviour.

Elmer took the lead but knew that it might not stay that way if Freya got wind of a likely den site. He trotted off with Freya close behind, followed quickly by Meg, with Buster bringing up the rear, to keep a protective eye on his sister.

The family had only covered a couple of miles when Freya slowed to a halt. She let out a low, quiet "woof", and Elmer turned to see her disappearing into the trees. Elmer followed her in while the pups heeded their fathers backward stare, and stayed on the path. Both pups knew their parents were investigating something and laid down, waiting happily to see what happened.

An abandoned foxes den had drawn Freya in, the scent of fox could still be smelt but it was old. A quick look around told Freya it might make a good starting point for a den of her own, so she took some time to inspect the ground more closely. This site was further from the river, but not that far, and sat on a slight incline. The vegetation around was quite sparse at the moment but it would soon fill in, making it harder for others to see. Freya made up her mind that this would make a good second den site, it was a couple of miles

161

from the other site and would not take too long to move the new pups here should something go wrong at the first site.

Elmer knew she had made a decision when Freya started marking all around it, he followed suit, laying his families claim to this area: the second den site had been chosen. Buster and Meg watched on keenly as their parents busied themselves checking the surrounding area, making it theirs. Both pups instinctively knew the reasons for it and took it as a reason to get a little excited, things would have got a lot more crazy had Meg been her usual self. Buster held back his bravado, just a bit.

With the formalities now over Freya wanted to head for her main den site and start work on it, she took the lead and headed straight there. As she travelled thoughts about how things had gone before trickled through her mind. Last year it was just her and Elmer, and she had wanted to do the entire den work herself. She now had a larger, stronger family behind her, and told herself that she would allow them to help this time. Things would still have to be done to her liking though.

The first densite area was as they had left it. A quick check of the immediate area revealed no signs to worry about. Elmer wanted to make sure and spent some time wandering around the immediate area, reinforcing his marks. A driven Freya started clearing around the new den entrance with gusto. Seasons of forest litter had covered and entered the old badger setts main entrance, Freya feverishly scraped it out and threw it back behind her. There were other entrances to the old sett that were also half buried but she would leave them alone, they only needed one way in and out. Meg watched her mother and found herself wanting to get involved, she took up a position behind Freya and joined in, throwing the detritus further down the slight incline, away from the den entrance; she was still aching from her recent injuries but felt impelled to help. There was not a lot for Elmer and Buster to do at the moment and Elmer's thoughts turned to patrolling their territory and reinforcing his families claim to it.

Buster, taking it upon himself, trotted off to a spot about ten yards above his mother and sister and found a small piece of flat ground on the slight hillside, it afforded him the perfect place to lay comfortably and keep an eye out from above them, so he settled in. Elmer knew he would stay there and watch over his family, that he would do his all to keep them safe, so he set off to patrol their land. Buster watched as his father melted away into the distance, strong inklings to follow made him fidgety, but he would always do his bit, with a tiny sigh he laid his head on his outstretched paws, to watch, smell and listen.

Elmer trotted steadily and easily along, stopping every few hundred yards to mark and scrape up the ground. He would have liked to have his son with him, together they were a potent force, but he also wanted his family to remain protected while he was away. He made his way to the river, following it to the top of their land. As he rounded a bend in the river some movement caught his eye, something was bobbing up and down in the water ahead of him. He stopped still to survey the scene.

It was an otter. He had seen them before but they were rare visitors here. Elmer had never come across any of the otters slimy, strong smelling droppings, usually left on raised marking places, and thought this male might be seeking out a new territory. Elmer watched from a distance, the otter still unaware of the wolf's eyes upon him.

The big, oily looking dog otter was well over a metre long, too big to be a sow, and he was a good fisherman, he had to be. The otter needed to eat well every day to keep it's almost constantly moving body in top condition, sometimes hunting for five hours a day, even longer if there were pups to feed.

Elmer watched the otter as he hunted the water, every time he resurfaced a high pitched whistle filled the air, the harder he worked the more he signalled. The otter dived down. Elmer waited almost motionless for three or four minutes, his eyes the only things moving as he scanned the surface, looking for it's reappearance. The hunter resurfaced, this time not whistling, he couldn't, for he was grappling with a trout half as long as himself.

The otter rolled quickly onto his back, struggling to hold the wriggling fish with all four webbed feet. The fish's tail was near the otter's head, so he speedily chewed it up; if he did loose his grip and drop the trout it would be unable to swim away. Frantic movements carried on as the trout was manoeuvred into a position that finally allowed the otter to bite the back of the fish's head, hard and fast, to kill it.

The trout was too big to eat while floating in the water so the otter swam to the bank towing its dead prey with it. He dragged it out of the water and half way up the stony bank. Sitting up on his hind feet and using his tail for extra balance the otter scanned the area all around, before settling back down to feed. He still hadn't seen Elmer. The otter should have gone to the top of the bank or stayed near the water but he was between the two. Unable to see clearly all around and too far from the water; he might have made a costly mistake.

The bank on this part of the river was higher than most other places and the ever opportunistic wolf saw a chance. Elmer moved in. The wind was in his favour, keeping his body as low as possible he went to his right and up over the bank, into dead ground that the otter couldn't see. Belying his large size Elmer moved quickly but quietly to a spot he thought in line with, and directly above his target. He was now in position. After inching slowly towards the top of the bank he stopped a few yards from it's crest to compose himself, preparing to rush forwards and over the top. Hopefully the otter was still there and would be taken by surprise.

The otter was caught out completely as Elmer burst over the bank top above him. The mustelid predator, eyes bulging out of his head at the sight before him, dropped his fish and turned his wiry body tightly, making a dash for the water. Elmer was close behind him but the slippery rocks gave him less grip than the otter, he stumbled heavily, his head going downwards as one of his front paws fell between two large rocks, forcing him to stop quickly: he didn't want to break a leg.

Just before Elmer looked back up he heard the loud 'plopping' noise as the fleeing otter dived blindly and unceremoniously into the water. Elmer scanned the water, there was just an outward wave of circular ripples to be seen.

All was not lost though. The otter had abandoned his substantial meal in his haste to escape, and not much of the large trout had been eaten. Elmer lay down, spreading himself out flat across a few rocks and pushing his nose down between them to try and grab the slippery fish that had fallen down there. After a few changes in position and stabs downwards with his nose, he managed to grasp it securely, hoisting it upwards. He would now enjoy a rare and tasty treat. For a moment Elmer thought about taking some back to the others, but it was not that big a fish for such a large wolf.

The unexpected meal was nearly all gone when the otter reappeared in the centre of the river, his head bobbing up and down as he watched the wolf eat his prize. He knew the wolf would have no chance of catching him in the water so he stayed for a while, chattering away, and observing him closely.

The fish was soon all eaten and Elmer looked straight at his benefactor, licking his lips, face and surrounding fur clean, nothing remained of it. In the future he would make a point of keeping his eye out for this water predator; there might be some worth in it for him. With no further interest in the otter Elmer set off. The otter tracked him from the centre of the water until Elmer reached the limits of his land and turned right, heading away from the river. A few loud chirping noises rang out from the river as the otter went off on his own way.

Elmer took his time to remark his favourite places: track convergences, the edge of open areas, and on top of obvious higher places, like mounds and big tree stumps. He found no new sign of intruders and after a few miles turned back towards his family.

As Elmer headed into the den site he could see his son lying above the others, still in the same position as he had left him. Freya and Meg had stopped digging and were resting near the den entrance. Buster's head turned to watch his father approach, his big blue eyes growing bigger and swishing tail becoming ever faster the closer he got. Eventually the desire was too much for him and he sprung up, trotting out happily to greet him.

Buster buried his head into Elmer's side and they enjoyed a playful little wrestle together, before the others came over to join them. A moment of joyful madness descended.

CHAPTER 29

LADY LUCK

Work on the new den was going well and Freya thought it was nearly finished. It had become the centre of the whole family's attention over the last few days and all, even Elmer, had done some digging on it. Elmer could see that Freya was happy with the way things were going and his thoughts turned to other things.

With little real work left to do on the den and so more time for Freya and Meg to keep their own wary eye out Elmer thought it would be safe to take Buster off hunting with him. Meg seemed almost back to her usual self but Elmer still worried about taking her on a hunt.

The family had not eaten for a few days and Buster needed little encouragement from his father to prepare himself to leave. Meg wanted to go too, she thought she was ready, but accepted the will of her father; staying with Freya to help her finish the den, and keep a watchful eye.

Elmer loved patrolling, hunting and just moving through his land, but he loved doing it even more when accompanied by his son. The bond between them was great and when with his son he felt capable of almost anything. He felt similar feelings for all his family but with Buster it was somehow a little different, just like he remembered it with his own father. Elmer knew that one day in the future Buster would leave to find his own place in this world, but until then, he would enjoy the time with him and the rest of his family, and do his best to prepare them for their life ahead. As they travelled Elmer spent some time reflecting on his feelings and times that he had with his own father, Orin.

Father and son moved like one through their scent filled land. The woodland plants were all flowering again, the strong smells attacking their delicate noses. All the trees were flourishing too, clothing themselves quickly with shiny new, bright green leaves. In just a few weeks time the canopy high above would fill in properly, cutting out most of the sunlight that managed to reach the forest floor, it would become darker and the short lived flowers that now carpeted it would quickly die away, not to be seen again for another year.

Elmer slowed and lowered his nose to the ground. Buster hung back watching as his father veered of the rough track they were on. Walking now, head still down, Elmer was on the trail of something. Buster followed him and could now smell the scent that held his fathers attention. The draw of this scent was strong. It was another wolf.

The single wolf track was over a day old and both followed it closely, hoping to find some sort of sign that would tell them more. Elmer knew a wolf travelling alone often moved without marking, especially when in the territory of others, the fear of discovery and the resulting aggression could sometimes be fatal: one's life was often risked though, if a wolf was being driven by the urge to find a mate.

Father and son converged on the same small tussock of grass, sniffing the area around it deeply. A lone female wolf had left her mark here, and both could tell from it that she was fit, healthy and of breeding age. Her time for breeding this year had already passed and she probably had not found herself a mate, otherwise she would be somewhere else with him, not in their territory. Her track was leading to the top of their land. Elmer gave his son a quick look, then trotted off at a faster pace.

The lone female would have known she was in the land of others, but had left her sign in the hope of enticing one of the resident males to seek her out. Elmer wanted to make sure she had left their land. Buster was intrigued by this females scent and he eagerly followed on, hoping they might just catch up with her.

The track was easy to follow and though they moved quickly her head start was too great. They soon reached the edge of their homeland and Elmer stopped abruptly. Buster came up beside him. Both peered onwards looking for any sign of movement. Elmer could sense the eagerness in his son and thought that maybe Buster wanted to carry on, he stepped forward, slightly blocking his path.

Buster knew himself that now was not his time, he still had much to learn and was too young to successfully breed, but he found the feelings deep within him, strange and compelling.

Elmer knew only too well what could happen when a wolf left his birth pack too early. In his own birth pack one of his brothers had left the family at an age even younger than Busters, in response to the innate draw of a passing female in breeding condition, he had followed her into a neighbouring packs land, and paid for it with his life.

Happy the female intruder had moved on Elmer turned and trotted off. Buster had one last look into the distance then turned too, quickly catching up to his father. They moved together again, happy and content.

The two patrolling wolves had not travelled far when some small movements caught the eye of Buster, he stopped to look in its direction. His nose worked hard to try and grab some scent but none was in the air. Elmer turned and headed back to his son, taking his place tall and serious looking beside him. A pile of leaves moved sharply, the rustling noises reverberating around the wolves sensitive ears, something was underneath them, both focused their attention towards it. The unseen creature was small whatever it was and an ever inquisitive Buster had to go and take a look.

As he padded towards the sounds the leaf litter suddenly erupted and a long thin creature shot out of it. Brown on the top, and white underneath, with a long tail that had a black tip to it, the small mammal moved with impressive, darting speed. The puzzled young wolf had never seen one of these before and for a split second thought about his reaction. The fast, jerky movements of the mammal made Buster's instincts kick in, and he was after it.

The stoat was fast, it turned sharply sending the much bigger and less agile young wolf barrelling past into a pile of leaves and twigs. Buster burst back up and was after it again. The little hunter covered the ground with a speed that belied its tiny size. Again Buster found himself overshooting the target to be left chewing on leaves and twigs.

Elmer was watching the scene before him with interest. Buster was not going to give up and the fleeing stoat now sensed this. Turning easily at speed the agile little predator made a dash for a

168

nearby oak tree, Buster right behind him. The well knurled bark of the forest giant gave the stoats sharp little claws plenty of grip, and the adept tree climber was up it in an instant; a regular treetop hunter of birds eggs and chicks, it came naturally to him.

Buster took a leap up the tree to follow but quickly realised tree climbing was not one of the wolfs strong points, and slid back to the ground. He stood up on his back legs and pushed his front paws as high up the tree as he could, looking for his tormentor. The little hunter was now sat safely out of reach on a large bow, peering down and hissing almost defiantly. Buster growled and barked upwards, but was more than a little put out as he returned to the ground, swung around and trotted back to his father.

Elmer had come across stoats before, but they were not seen often. In harsh snow time winters their coats often turned completely white, making them even harder to see. He knew well how hard they were to catch and often it was more for the fun of the chase than anything else that a wolf would interact with them, he did though have some sort of respect for these fearless little killers, before now he had wondered what the outcome might be if they were a much bigger animal.

The pair set of again. Elmer headed for an area that he knew often held fallow deer mothers at this time of year. The female deer were still a few weeks away from having their fawns and they often herded together in groups for protection. When the fawns did arrive Elmer and his family would be regular visitors to these areas.

His knowledge was sound, there were a few deer in the area, but straight away Elmer could tell something was different. All the deer seemed very alert, they always were, but today they seemed even more so: he worried that another predator had already been around. Buster was eager to get hunting, his lack of experience was not telling him the same story as his father.

Elmer began to move with more stealth, like he did when he was looking for something that wasn't prey. Buster realised now that something was amiss, he could see the change in his father's movements and the thoughts of a hunt were pushed quickly to the back of his mind. Both wolves now moved slowly and quietly, constantly sniffing the air and occasionally stopping to maximise their hearing.

Something was moving ahead of them, Elmer heard it first, and stopped dead in his tracks, massive head fixed forwards. Buster stood alert and still behind him, his ears swivelling from side to side in a bid to hear something too. 'Crunch!' The sound of snapping twigs were easily heard by both wolves and they froze, waiting statue like for the culprit to come into view.

The male brown bear was two years old, thin and weak. He had gone into hibernation barely heavy enough to survive it and since emerging had found little to eat. Six months earlier he had still been with his mother and sibling and not far from denning when they were attacked by a giant, rogue male bear. His sister was killed first and then his mother too, as she tried courageously to defend them. The young bear, still not fully prepared for a life alone, was forced to flee for his life, and later to den on his own. He walked unaccompanied now through the young grass and bracken looking for fawns, but he was far too early for that.

Elmer and Buster watched closely as he ambled into view, both could tell he was young, his low weight and slightly dishevelled appearance told them also that he was probably weak and inexperienced. Although no real threat to them he had to be sent on his way, he was heading in the direction of the new den; no chances could be taken.

Father and son headed straight towards the young bear, they made no attempt to hide themselves and he saw them quickly. The youngster didn't want to fight and moved quickly away. Elmer had no intention of actually fighting this bear, there was no immediate reason too, no kill, den or pups to protect, he would just be happier if this hungry bear moved on.

Elmer and Buster took up positions side by side between the bear and their distant den, moving forwards and forcing the bear to retreat away from them. The young bear got the message and turned tail, running away. Father and son followed the bear for a distance, keeping him moving and only backing off a little as they approached the river boundary. The juvenile bear easily swam across. Elmer and his son watched on, as dripping wet the bear left the river and shook himself dry on the far bank. He gave a quick look over his shoulder back towards the pair of wolves then set off into another's land.

170

They had done a good job so far today, keeping their land safe, but Elmer didn't want to go back to Freya with no food today. He headed for another area that on occasion also held some deer, Buster happily and eagerly following on.

It took a few miles of purposeful trotting to get there. On arrival they slowed and searched for signs of prey. There were some deer about and though they were their normal, highly vigilant selves, Buster could tell the difference between the usual alertness of these and the ones they had just encountered around the bear. He had learnt another lesson; if your prey seems more jumpy and uneasy than expected then there is probably a reason for it.

Elmer concentrated his gaze on a small group of three deer. Buster could tell he had picked them out. The undergrowth was still not at its highest but it did offer some concealment and they both moved towards them. The deer stood together in a fairly open area, it would make it difficult to get close. Father and son split apart and each made their way slowly down opposite sides of the group.

The direction of the wind was such that it would soon take Elmer's scent to them. He decided to rush in. They could have done with Freya or Meg's speed here but he hoped that one might make a mistake and allow him or his son to benefit.

Buster heard and then saw his father making a move, he responded by rushing in himself. The browsing deer were caught unawares to start, but the most experienced of the group kept her calm for a second and quickly saw the way out. She ran straight ahead and out the top of the trap with her two companions close behind. Had Freya been here she would probably have been able to close this avenue of escape but neither Elmer nor Buster were fast enough.

Elmer and Buster may not have been quicker than the female deer but their stamina was better, they could keep up a good speed for some distance. Both came together behind the fleeing deer and pursued them. The ground cover was becoming thicker and more tangled, it hindered these smaller deer. Father and son were not really closing but they kept the pressure on, Elmer hoping that one might trip or even better injure itself in the panic of the chase, and allow them to take the advantage.

171

One of the deer was not as fast as the others and it veered off onto its own path, hoping to split the wolves. It didn't work. Elmer and Buster both followed the single doe, each seeing some sort of desperation in her tactics. Still pursuing and keeping up the pressure, they both waited for the deer to make some kind of mistake.

Father and son were feeling the strain of the long pursuit as there lungs worked overtime to grab in huge mouthfuls of air, legs were starting to feel heavy and slow and both were starting to think this hunt might not be a winnable one, when luck took a turn in their favour.

The deer was working to her extreme too, she was well aware of the wolves still on her tail and moved swiftly with the promise of further life driving her on. Her small hooves and thin legs were sinking deep into the thick undergrowth while the wolves much larger paws squashed some of it flat. She was using a little more energy and getting tired, finding it harder to concentrate on placing her feet safely. Moving flat out she didn't see the old burrow entrance hidden below years of decaying forest material, one of her front legs went down it, she stumbled heavily and her shoulder impacted the ground with bone breaking force, spinning her over and over.

Lady luck had indeed smiled on them today. Elmer's family would eat well tonight.

CHAPTER 30

THE SECOND DENSITE

Elmer and his family had spent the last week in the vicinity of the new den. Freya was getting restless, she wanted to go to the second den site and get it ready. Elmer could see the uneasiness within her and knowing she wanted to move he padded over to reassure her that they would soon be leaving. Gently but firmly he pushed his large wet nose into her side, running it along her body, up to her head, finishing with a head rub and a low, contented whine.

Buster and Meg watched their parents closely, experts now in the body language of wolves both knew they would soon be moving off, a quick bout of play wrestling seemed to be called for. Meg was growing stronger and faster by the day and could once again easily evade Buster's advances, if she wanted too. Elmer left Freya's side and trotted over to the pups, he stopped just short of them to stretch, but it quickly turned into a deep play bow, the result seeing him pile in for some serious ruff and tumble. Freya watched her family play for a short time, eventually getting to her feet and carrying out her own, less intense stretches.

Freya took the lead, heading for the old foxes den that had been chosen weeks before, she moved with an urgency that was obvious to the rest of her family. Elmer and the pups trailed along happily behind her.

In the few short weeks since Freya and Elmer had last been there Mother Nature had done her thing and changed the surrounding lands appearance. Bluebells, Anemones, Sorrels, different forest grasses, brackens and ferns, now covered the woodland floor. Freya left the faint path and headed through the strong smelling flora to the den area. It was about fifty yards from the path.

All the family followed her in, splitting up on arrival to do their own checking out of the surrounding area. Elmer moved furthest afield while Buster and Meg stayed closer to the den and Freya.

A short time later Elmer was back. Freya didn't want to wait any longer and straight away started to clear the entrance. Buster and Meg felt driven to help her but with no room beside her decided to scrape and clean the immediate ground around the entrance area, clearing this seemed a natural instinct to them; it would allow easier sighting of smaller threats close to the new pups, dangers like snakes, that might hide in and move through any near vegetation. The plants a little further away would be left untouched, to help hide the site from more distant prying eyes. Elmer found himself a good position about fifty yards away and settled down to keep a watchful eye out.

A few hours in and Freya was making her way slowly into the old fox den widening it as she went, Buster was now behind her using his youthful enthusiasm, strength and huge paws to easily fling the excavated soil back behind him towards Meg, who busily and not really knowing why, spread it about the den entrance.

Elmer thought he should get involved now and came over to take a look. Buster and Meg stopped their work and greeted him with their usual excited squeals, head rubs and face licking. Freya carried on digging. Elmer turned from his excited pups and peered into the den. Freya was throwing pawfuls of soil underneath and behind her, he thought better of interrupting her for now, and anyway the tunnel still looked a bit small for him. He would let the others carry on digging it for now, when he came back later for another look it might be bigger. Elmer turned and after a quick nudge into his pups, returned to his position of guardian.

It was late afternoon and Freya decided that enough digging had been done for today. She backed up out of the den and after a quick look towards Buster and Meg headed over to Elmer and fell into his side. Brother and sister watched as their parents enjoyed rolling around together. The pups decided they would leave mum and dad to it, a few heavy nudges and excited growls to build the mood, and they tore off to explore the land around the densite further.

Brother and sister were revelling in each others company, especially Meg now she had her speed back. Wrestling and enjoying spurts of chasing each other through the forest were top of the list for now. They ran flat out, shoulder to shoulder, barging each other sideways, one would stop and let the other catch hold of them, and a play fight would follow; as always Buster held back some of his power so that Meg wouldn't give up.

Spring was in full flow now, every time the happy duo stopped to wrestle large patches of fresh forest flowers and bright green foliage were flattened beneath them; leaving a sure sign to any that they had been around.

Elmer lay close beside Freya thinking about the pups that would soon be joining their family, enjoying the feelings. Freya was dozing off and as Elmer cast his pleasured gaze over her he thought about his mates recent changes in behaviour. Lately he had noticed some subtle differences in her, ones that he liked, slowly she was becoming just a little more softer and tolerant: he pondered why.

As Elmer thought about his partner he also listened to his youngsters playing in the distance, swivelling his ears around he took in their excited growls and playful barks, a picture of their distant antics took form in his mind, making him feel even happier.

Dusk was approaching and the whole family were back together near the den. Freya still had work to do, the entrance tunnel needed expanding further and the area at the end of it, where she would lay with the pups, still needed to be dug. This time she would make the family area a little larger, to give enough room for her or any visiting adults to turn around and go back out head first. Work would carry on tomorrow.

Half way through the next day the second den site was completed. Freya was happy with the final result, she knew it would make a good second home if something was to happen at her first choice. Freya had learnt from the harsh lessons of last year, the experiences of her first time as a mother had been taken in, she would do her utmost to make sure that things went better this year.

Freya knew her time was getting closer and Elmer seemed to know it too. He could sense the hormonal changes taking place within her and could see the subtle differences in her behaviour. Buster and Meg were also aware some new pups would soon be joining their family, both were becoming just a little more excited every day, as the time grew nearer.

The family laid together around the completed second den site for a few hours until Freya got purposely to her feet. Elmer followed suit, he knew where they would be heading and went over to get the youngsters ready to move. Freya stretched her body out with slow, long, drawn out movements, not wanting to move too quickly, while Elmer and the pups used some vigorous play to warm themselves up.

Ready now, Freya caught the eye of her partner. She looked at him hard, letting him know it was time to go, and without any further ado she set off. Elmer broke off his play with Buster and Meg, a quick energetic body shake followed then he trotted off too, taking his place behind her. Buster and Meg played together for a little longer before finally pulling apart, both had a good shake, just like their father, then ran to catch up with their fast disappearing parents.

The whole family were soon back at the main den site. After a quick look around to make sure all was well Freya lay gently down, her eyes inviting Elmer to nuzzle her, they enjoyed a close moment while Buster and Meg went into play mode again. Meg was getting extra excited, it seemed that since her close shave with the big male Lynx she had found again her true love of play with her big brother, and she welcomed it. Freya would stay around the den site now until it was time to go in and have her pups. It would not be long.

The next morning came. Buster was lying wide awake in the same position that he had taken up days before, when he had watched over his mother and sister as they dug the den out. It was a good position to see from, just a few metres further up the slight incline, above the den, allowing a view of all below. Only an intruder approaching the den from much higher up would not easily be seen, but hopefully the heavy forest vegetation there would allow any such to be heard. For the near future this would be Buster's place and he would only move from it to urinate and defecate: he had made himself guardian and relished the opportunity to do his bit.

Elmer would always be around but with his large and capable son watching over Freya and the den he could concentrate his efforts further afield, to keep their homeland safe and keep them fed. Meg, now almost completely back to herself, would split her time between being at the den site with her brother, and starting to accompany Elmer on his travels.

Freya could feel the familiar movements within her. She shuffled around frequently, trying to find the most comfortable position. Elmer and the others knew it would not be long now and were not surprised when Freya got meaningfully to her feet. After a quick look around the family and a nudge into Elmer's side she headed into the den. Freya moved along the short tunnel, laying herself down in the larger area at it's end, made for her and the pups. She waited, for the waves of pain that would soon be coming.

CHAPTER 31

NEW LIFE COMES AND GOES

Freya had been in the den all morning. The waves of pain surged through her body more regularly now, she prepared herself for the first arrival.

Elmer and Meg lay at the entrance of the den looking into it, both temporarily detached from the world around them. Buster was in his lookout position, but the urge to know what was going on grew evermore unbearable, it finally became too much and he made his way down to the others. Piling into his sisters side she answered him with a quick snap of her jaws telling him that this was not the time for play, 'they were listening!'

Buster settled down beside Meg and his father, the three of them stretched out, side by side. Every time a noise came from the den their heads would angle around in unison and their tails would start swishing slowly from side to side, trying to hear better what was happening below ground.

Another hour passed and Freya could feel the first pup coming, she got into the most comfortable position she could and almost immediately the first pup, a male, burst its way into the world. Reassuring little squeals came almost immediately from the tiny new arrival. Freya knew what to do and quickly pulled the sac from around him and ate it, she then licked him clean. Just like last years pups the blind and death little bundle instinctively gravitated towards her bodily warmth and nestled in.

Outside, at the den entrance, the others all sprang to their feet, a chorus of excitable sounds filling the air as they bounced around. Buster knocked Meg over as he barged heavily into her side and she jumped back up snapping wildly at the air around him. Elmer strutted around rubbing his head and side into the others then dived on his back and rolled violently on the forest floor, all the time little whines, whimpers and howls of excitement coming from him.

The first pup didn't have time to get settled in for the second pup was not far behind. Freya jerked herself around, depositing him squirming and helpless on the den floor; even though his mother was only inches away he kicked up a mighty little fuss. Freya found it hard, but she ignored his whining for now, getting on with what she had to do.

The second pup, like the first, came quickly into the world. It was a female and noticeably much quieter than her just born brother, Freya was sure she was fine though, just much calmer. Freya cleaned her up and then brought the two pups together with gentle pushes of her nose. Huddling together in the safety of their mothers side they both searched blindly and instinctively for a teat, but they wouldn't have time to find one. Freya could feel the last pup moving around within her and it wasn't going to wait. She was to have three pups again: their family would now be seven strong.

Freya moved a little slower this time, letting the first two pups roll less hard onto the den floor. Both still let out little yelps as they landed but Freya didn't have time to comfort them. The third pup was another male. He was the biggest and took much longer than the other two to push out, there were no problems though, and after cleaning and stimulating him she now had three loud, healthy new pups wriggling around before her.

She cast her motherly gaze over her charges. Like all newborn wolf pups they were all varying degrees of darkness in colour, the largest male was quite big but she thought nowhere near as big as Buster had been, he was the darkest in colour with no other visible markings. The other male was smaller but still quite a bit bigger than the female pup and not as dark as the big pup. The female pup was the lightest in colour of the three, the smallest and the quietest, but Freya seemed somehow to already sense that she would become a bold wolf.

Freya quickly cleaned up the den floor, eating any afterbirth and eliminations, then settled down to give her pups their first proper feed. Laying beside them she guided her charges to the right spot with more gentle nudges of her cold wet nose. After a bit of blind squabbling and kneading of her stomach with uncontrolled little legs they all latched on and a near silence descended. All that could be

179

heard was contented moans as the fragile new pups had their first of mothers milk.

Back above ground the mood was one of elation as the whole family whooped and whined. Elmer wanted to go and take a look, the urge was great but he would wait this year, he knew now that this was Freya's time and that she would invite him in when the time was right. Buster and Meg, especially Buster, were also keen to take a look at the new arrivals but seeing their father holding back they followed his lead; they would wait until their parents thought the time was right.

Hours later and Elmer was still charged by the birth of his latest pups, deciding to redirect that energy into searching for some prey. His outward appearance changed quickly to one that Buster and Meg knew well and Elmer gave Meg the look she had been waiting for; she prepared to move off with her father. Buster knew he was going to stay and watch over Freya and the pups, and happily trotted off, tail swishing from side to side, up to his lookout position.

Elmer watched briefly as his son took his place above the den. He could make out Buster's bright blue eyes moving slowly around in his formidable head, scanning the forest. Elmer knew he could go off hunting, safe in the knowledge that Buster would give his life in the protection of Freya and their new pups. He turned and set off with Meg close behind, the combination of Elmer's strength and his daughter's now returned speed would make them a potent hunting force. Until now Buster and Meg had not contributed much to the actual hunt, but Elmer thought that as they now had new mouths to feed it was time for them to start taking a much more active roll: they were not the youngest pups any more.

Freya was resting now, the birth of the pups had been quick but it had still taken a lot out of her. With the pups laying warm, safe and well fed against her she tried to relax. As the pups dozed they let out little moans as a sign of their contentedness, this told Freya that all was well and she need not bother them. Sometimes they would emit little growls when huddled together, more a sign of togetherness at this time of life, growls would take on other meanings as they grew older. Freya remembered these behaviours from her pups of last year and enjoyed watching it all again.

Every few minutes one of the pups would stir and set the others off, and a bout of mutual yawning, squealing and moaning followed, with the occasional yelp if one of them thought the occasion required it. Freya always responded to the more serious screams or yelps by giving some attention, gently nudging or repositioning the pup with her nose.

Elmer and Meg moved confidently along, Meg had not hunted alone with her father before; she would enjoy and learn from the experience. They were only a few miles from the den when Elmer came to a halt, raising his nose high into the air and sniffing hard.

The forest floor was now thicker with ferns and brackens, some higher than the wolf was tall, the tree canopy was also starting to close in, making it darker. The wolf's eyesight was more limited in this lower light and heavier foliage and so their sense of smell became even more prominent and important.

Meg raised her head too, she couldn't smell anything yet but she followed her father's example and scented the air with purpose. Elmer headed into the thicker brush, he moved slowly and deliberately. Meg followed him in and now knew what he was looking for; she prepared herself to run.

The fallow deer fawn was over four weeks old and should really have already been out moving around with his mother by now. The doe had left the fawn in the broad leaved bracken while she went off to feed, returning periodically to nurse and check on him. The mother would do this until she thought he was capable of keeping up with her and escaping predators.

The fawn pushed himself down as low as possible and froze as he heard something that wasn't his mother approaching. Concealment and quietness were his best defence but if it failed he was already capable of running quite well. He would wait until the final moment before taking off.

Meg moved away from Elmer as they approached the well hidden fawn in line abreast. Both were moving dead slow, their eyes now coming more to the fore as they peered into the greenness, looking for any movement ahead of them.

The frightened fawn could hear the thumping of his own heartbeat in his ears and feel the flight hormones welling up within him, priming him with the fuel that he would need. He could sense the approaching wolves but couldn't see them yet and raised himself only slightly to allow for a quicker take off.

Meg moved just like her mother, Elmer glanced over and for a split second thought he might be hunting with Freya. Meg was only feet from the hidden fawn now as she too went through her own last preparations for a chase. She focused her mind, the untapped energy building up within her was waiting to be released and she told herself on the first sign of movement she would go.

The fawn saw her first and in one swift movement rose up, turned, and exploded away from her.

Meg was more than ready. She shot forwards and was quickly on the fawn's tail. The long, gripping vegetation, severely hampered the fawns speed as he dodged and weaved quickly in a bid to escape his pursuer. Meg closed on the young fawn, had the young deer been able to reach more open ground it might have had a chance but in the long bracken and grasses it's fate was sealed. Meg tripped the fawn just like she used to when playing with Buster, and it was all over.

Meg was happy with the way her own first hunt had gone. Elmer was happy too, he had let Meg do it all herself as the prey was easy and not dangerous, the experience would be good for her. Elmer approached Meg's kill and without question she relinquished it to him. He opened the carcass and the twenty pounds of meat was quickly consumed by both of them.

Minutes later, meal finished, Elmer moved off again, they would carry on the search for some larger prey, if none was to be found they could still regurgitate some of the meat for Freya and Buster back at the den.

As they left the waiting ravens came down. There was nothing left for them but still they squabbled.

CHAPTER 32

CONTEMPLATION

The new pups were two weeks old now, their eyes and ears only recently opened. Their immediate world was now a much more interesting and informative place to them as they explored the den and its entrance. They could now associate properly to things they previously just smelt and touched.

Elmer was near the den entrance when one of the male pups put in its first appearance. He went straight over, then gently smelt and nudged him. The little pup sensed something about this giant wolf before him and rolled onto his back in an innate show of submission. Elmer licked and rolled him gently over as the pup touched him with his little paws. The pup got clumsily back to his feet then licked and nudged around Elmer's head as his father pushed it into him. Elmer could hear the other pups further in the den and found the draw was too much for him. He went in, the pup instinctively following him. Freya was laid at the end of the den with the other two pups and she gave him a welcoming look. Elmer wasted no time in nuzzling his partner, then said his first hello to his other pups.

Buster had left his position as lookout and now stood at the den entrance, Meg by his side, their tails wagging broadly while whining and growling in excitement at the smells and sounds making their way out of the den; but they would not go in.

Elmer spent only a few minutes in the den, enjoying being with the new pups and Freya. For him, this was the one of the best times. The pups were getting a bit too excited and he took it as his cue to leave. He turned and headed out of the den to be greeted by his other, older youngsters. Buster and Meg could smell the scent of the pups on their father and their feelings became even more intense, but still they would not go in the den. All the pups would soon be putting in appearances at the den entrance and they would be able to meet them then.

A bout of rough wrestling and full on chasing ensued as Elmer, Buster and Meg expended the joyous, pent up energy within them. Freya and the pups could hear the others outside playing hard, the pups listened intently, their new senses soaking things up like a sponge, it was the first time they had heard real growling and other adult vocalisations, their little heads twisted and turned as they took it all in; they were fascinated.

Over the next week the pups often made their way to the den entrance, drawn by the outside light and the opportunity to explore their immediate surroundings with their fast developing new senses. Whenever a pup did make it to the outside world they and any adults present were quick to interact and have some fun.

Buster would often leave his lookout position to play with one of the pups when they appeared, he loved it and all the pups seemed to be instantly drawn to him, this huge brother of theirs that was always about and would give his life in the protection of them or any of his family, already the little pups seemed to sense his strength and reliability.

Meg too loved to be around the pups. Soon the new arrivals would be spending more time outside the den entrance making it easier to have access to them. Being around the pups was bringing some strange feelings out from deep within her.

Freya wanted to bring all three pups out of the den today. They were three weeks old now and capable of spending more time outside the den entrance, she wanted them to start interacting more with the rest of the family and their surroundings. Freya got their attention by standing up quickly, the suddenness of it had all the pups eyes glued to her and with a purposeful look about her she trotted quickly out of the den; the pups would instinctively follow any adult that walked with purpose before them, and so they trailed out behind her.

All the family were waiting for them and the pups instantly became the centre of attention. A composition of excitable sounds filled the air as the whole family expressed their joy. The pups were just a bit cautious to start with but they soon worked out that they could get away with a lot, and some sort of mayhem followed.

Buster, like the rest of the family, happily let the pups crawl all over him, he could be seen strutting around the den site with one or two of them hanging like large chestnuts from his ears. Meg enjoyed playing with them too but the pups seemed to notice her slightly less forgiving ways, making a tolerant Buster more often the object of their attention.

Freya settled down to rest and watch her family play. Elmer stole himself away from the rejoicing to join her. The two of them laid tightly beside each other and together enjoyed watching the antics of their pups, both young and old, before them.

The new father cast his large amber eyes slowly around his family. Elmer watched his older pups playing with the new, the good thoughts and feelings welling up from deep inside him. Buster, the bravest and boldest of wolves, had made himself the protector of their new pups. Elmer knew that he would give his all to keep them safe. Meg, just like her mother, was sleek, fast and sometimes as stubborn, with more experience she would become an excellent hunter too, helping to provide well for their growing pack. Finally he looked towards his partner beside him, Freya, the mother of all his amazing pups, a slender wolf that was also fast and fearless, and of late, more open and forgiving. He now knew beyond doubt that family was everything to the wolf, that and a good homeland.

Elmer thought deeply about his first year as a breeding male with a territory and pack of his own, and wondered what the next year might bring. He would do all within his power to keep his pack safe, to ensure that they would always be well fed, with a land that was theirs and theirs alone. He would pass on all that he had learnt to his kin, so they could all thrive, and ultimately have families of their own. For Elmer was no ordinary wolf.

A wolf is not supposed to be alone.

Printed in Great Britain
by Amazon